AF444262

Yves Kerdal

Stubborn Survival

HR

First published in Great Britain in 2020 by Heggerwood Realms

Copyright © Yves Kerdal 2020

The moral right of Yves Kerdal to be identified as the author of this work has been asserted in accordance with the Copyright, Designs and Patents Act of 1988

All rights reserved. No part of this publication may be reproduced, stored in a retrieval system, or transmitted in any form, or by any means (electronic, mechanical, photocopying, recoding, or otherwise) without the prior written permission of both the copyright owner and the publisher of this book.

All the characters in this book, except for those already in the public domain, are fictitious, and any resemblance to actual persons living or dead is purely coincidental.

Front cover: Aude-Noëlle Nevius

Typeface: Garamond 11pt

ISBN-9798609868299

Dedicated to all Celts past and present, and in particular for those working towards a global reconciliation, for we have the same "Love of our Bloodline", Gwad Kerentez in Breton.

Acknowledgements

John Royal Horton, who prompted me to write the story of my people.

The late Peter Martin, for his encouragement.

Rachel Bonde, my kind editor for her insightful knowledge and patience.

Aude Nevius, for her gracious help with the design.

The people of Plumelec.

Last but not least, Margot Snowdon my wife who gave me the confidence to carry on with my project.

Author's Note

For a long time, I felt compelled to write a story on a topic not well known to many—the migration of the Celts of western England to Armorica, present day Brittany; it lasted from AD 400 until AD 600. Chronicles of their resettlements are sparse; passing of knowledge, mostly oral. I decided to go ahead and put ideas to paper. I realised the last vast movement of people was only a stage into the bigger history of Celtic migrations since 1000 BC. I also become conscious the passage to Brittany was not the end of the historical annals, I had to relate it to an utopian idea; the western Celts had bonds and a common need to get closer. This book is a saga, where truth and legend meet and where my spirit as a Celtic Breton expresses deep seated feelings and dreams.

The Celtic record is fragmented both in terms of an historical sense and geographically. Modern Celts often keep this spirit of fragmentation. I feel it is a grand misdeed to see these nations apart; it was not the case many centuries ago. It is also a great shame Celts fought for different masters during the Hundred Years War, Waterloo, the American Civil War, and more recently, in the Hibernian Gaelic fights. They fought each other for political and religious reasons, ignoring their common blood.

This book attempts to reduce the confusion which currently exists on the Celtic civilisation and hopes to show where common roots existed from the start of their migration westward in 800 BC, through to 700.

They left present day Bohemia, Southern Eastern Germany, and the Hartz mountains and went to what is now France, Switzerland, Belgium, Holland, Galicia (North West Spain) and Northern Italy. In turn, some travelled to what is now the British Isles from France, and Belgium. Others went from Galicia to Erin (Ireland) in 400 BC; from there they colonised part of Alba (Scotland).

In a twist of circumstance, some came back to France from Wales, the Scottish Borders and Cornwall, into Brittany in AD 400 to AD 700. Emigration movements also went East. The way they act today is the result of what has been passed along in their genes for centuries. Celtic blood is preponderant in France, predominant in Wales, Brittany, Ireland, Scotland, Nova Scotia, Newfoundland, Australia, and New Zealand, yet sparse in Switzerland and Galicia.

The ancestral languages are dying. Brittany and Ireland have the most speakers of a Celtic language. The Irish and the Scots speak a tongue derived from the Goidelic group of Celtic languages, whereas the Bretons, Welsh and Cornish originated from the Brythonic.

The image of the boorish Celt warrior guided by his impulses does not do justice to the sophistication of Celtic science which surprised even the Romans. The Celts related to the planets, especially the sun and the solstices. It was so vital to them, it directed their lives, especially where to settle and do battle.

Times for coming together are here again; cultural rapprochements are blossoming. It matters not if some of them remain under tutelage of their past conquerors. They know the spirituality, which is theirs, will never die.

Place Names in Antiquity	Modern Place Names
Aleth	St Malo
Alba	Scotland
Autricum	Chartres
Bareuth	Bayeux
Big Island	Great Britain
Big Rock	Ar Bras Roch
Braetoll	Bristol
Breizh / Little Britain	Brittany (in Breton) / Brittany
Breton Sea	English Channel
Bro-Dreger	Tregor
Broellian	Broceliante Forest-Brittany
Caerhix	Carhaix
Caerwick	Carlisle
Cricklade	Wiltshire
Cumbria	Cumberland
Cymru	Wales
Domenea Kingdom	Cornwall, Cumberland, Devon, Dorset, Gloustershire, Shropshire, Somerset
Dorsetshire	Dorset
Dumnonia	Devon
Dunnleann	Dublin
Erin	Ireland
Felgor	Fougeres
Finnygook	Crafthole-Cornwall
Gwenaber	Weymouth
Gwened	Vannes
Gwenporz	Whitehaven
Kemper	Quimper
Kernow	Cornwall
Landreger	Treguier
Lundun	London

Moraber	Morlaix
Mordon	Margate
Oceanus Germanicus	North Sea
Penaravon	Cremyll (Cornwall)
Penniorcoches	Pennines
Raoned	Rennes
Sabrina	Severn
Sulis	Bath
Tamesas	Thames
Treveleg	Plumelec
Waen	Vannes

DOMENEA KERNOW
BRITTANY
Erwan (brother)
Garoch
Bridgid
Konan
FIRST COUSINS
Annick
Cranadh
Gwen (1st wife)
Big Island
Ropaz
Ervar (Bohemia)
Morgana
Bodeca
Gerdan
Gralon
Meire
Marthod
FIRST COUSINS
Hildana
Brennus
Billig
GRANDSONS OF HEWL
FIRST COUSINS
Siebann
Hewl
Dann
Sizum
(Treveleg)
Artoad
Fanac (soldier)
Gaelb (granddaughter)
Armorica
650 BC
AD 400
AD 450
AD 500
AD 550
AD 600
AD 650

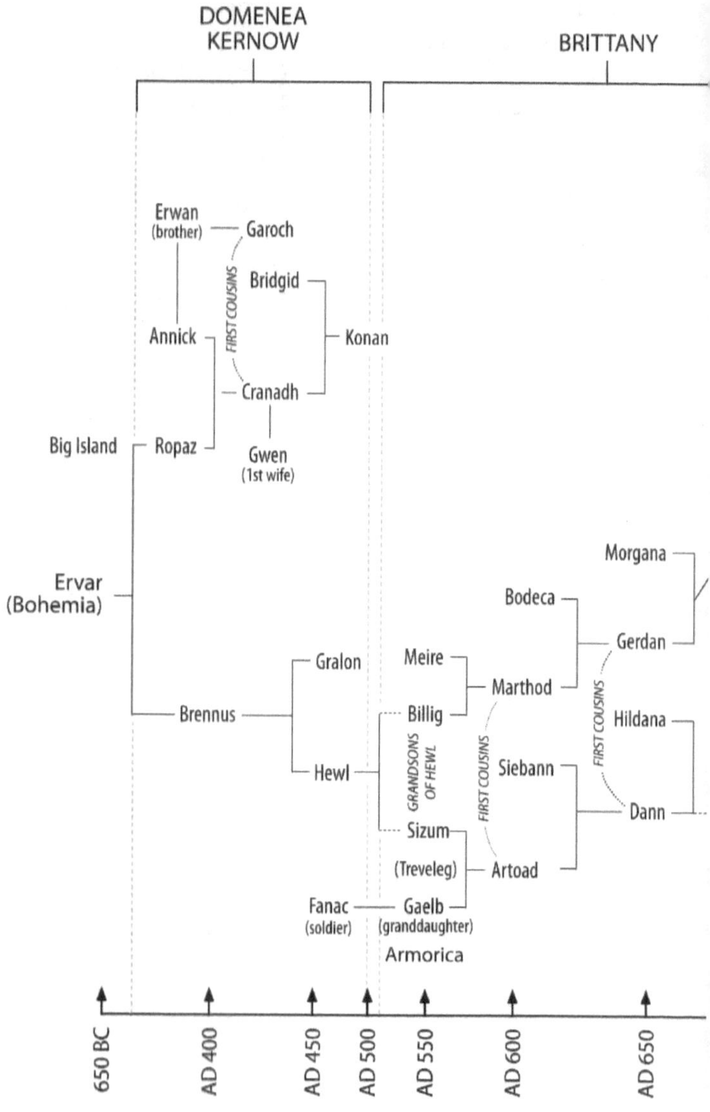

x

STUBBORN SURVIVAL

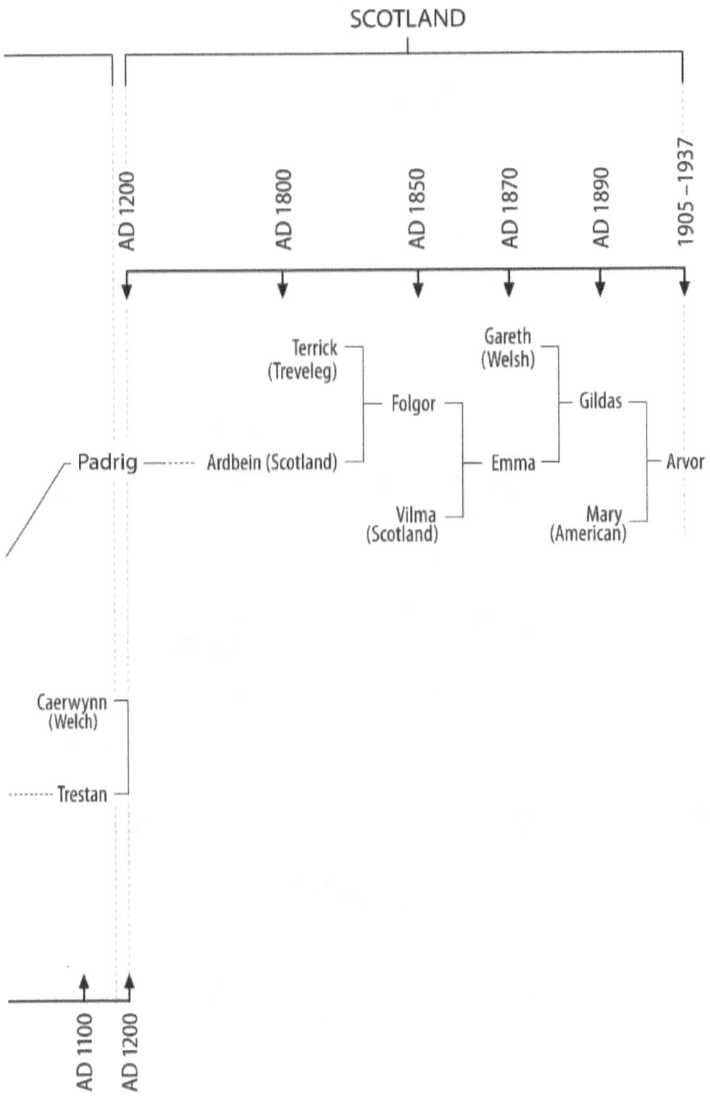

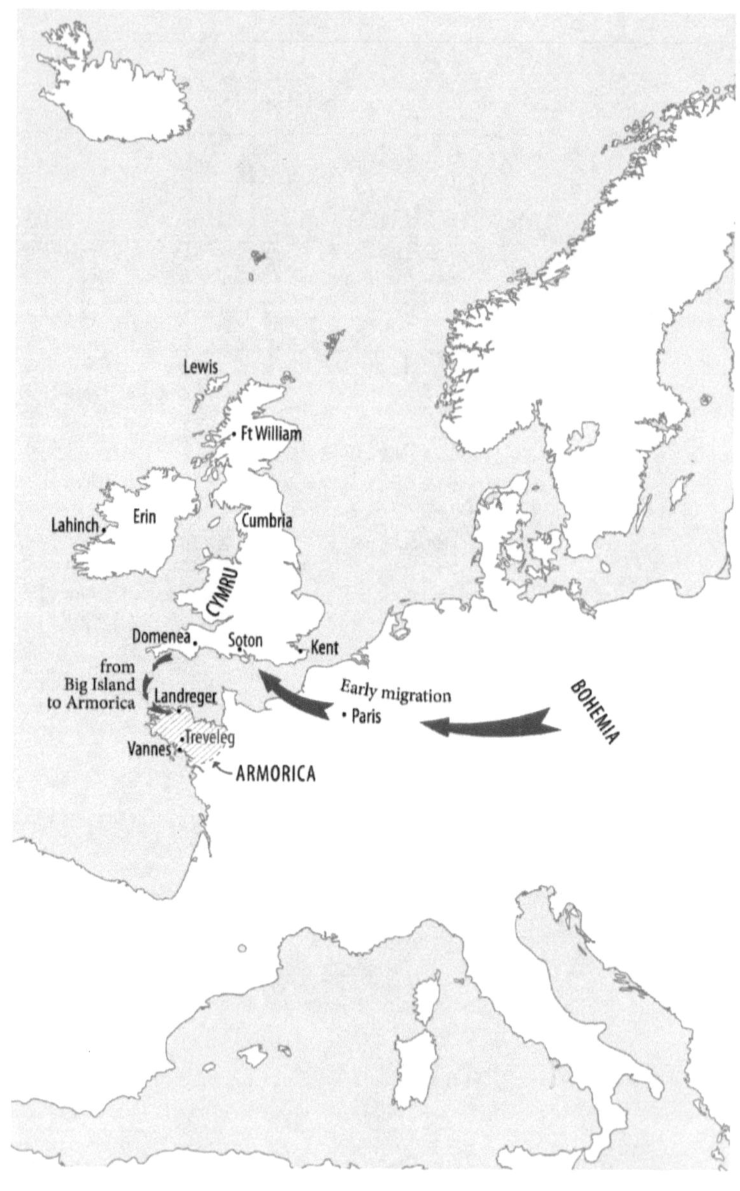

Lewis
Ft William
Lahinch
Erin
Cumbria
CYMRU
Domenea
Soton
Kent
from Big Island to Armorica
Landreger
Early migration
Paris
BOHEMIA
Treveleg
Vannes
ARMORICA

Chapter One

A long line of humans and animals was on the move; it stretched so far, the front could not be seen for it was beyond a small hill on the horizon where the sun sets. Ervar, the last person in the column, felt compelled to look behind him; he sighed, then turned around, looked forward to his tribe, and resumed walking. He had good reason to look back, the smell of burning bodies still hung in the air.

Twenty people had been sacrificed to the gods of the "land beyond life". Those chosen had been selected from the noble cast of the Kaerdalh tribe; they were vital in guaranteeing the unprecedented mission successful. The "Twenty" had climbed inside the giant straw statue and burned alive. Ervar could still hear their cries of desperation and their bodies moving frantically reacting to the agonising pains of their last instants. He was their leader and had ordered the gift to the gods. He would forever see these ten men and ten women walking in silence, emotionless on the ramp leading to the inside of their tomb. It was a ritual and the whole tribe had watched, humming incantations to the gods. The sacrifice was the biggest they had ever offered any deity as far back as tribal memories extended. For the martyrs it was not an issue of being willing or reluctant; they always knew since youth they could be called upon for the supreme surrender. The terror of a painful death made them walk with trembling legs and loss expressions on their faces. The remaining tribe members stood silent and stoic feel at the sight of their fellow kinsfolks enduring such a horror in the name of gratifying the gods.

The initial phase of the colossal exodus had been planned many months before, yet the ramifications of the spiritual aspect were still not resolved. Consciences were troubled; doubts were prevalent in the minds of the chief, the ruling council and the druids' cast. Their inner thoughts battled between the dictate of day-to-day living and the gods' commandments. The needs of the present had won, but they had to appease the "other world" the human offerings linked the earthly deed with the sacred realm.

As tribal chief, Ervar felt his shoulders insufficient to carry such a huge burden of immense responsibility.

The column extended the length of six hundred chariots. They were supposed to meet with another tribe, the Brae, in a day or so, and Ervar considered the obligation of leading his people from the front. Armed men and women were equally divided between the front, middle, and rear. His tribe, the Kaerdalh, formed part of the massive migration of Celtic people, moving to where the sun goes down.

The gods were unseen players of this colossal stirring. The druids had conferred in secret gatherings with the deities in the heavens; the latter had not agreed with the choice to leave. The tribe had inhabited their ancestral home as long as anyone could remember; it was sacred ground and leaving it was bound to upset some, if not all of the gods. The apprehension a spell would be cast upon the tribe gave cause to the "Curse of the Rhoem"— meaning unpredictable occurrences of adverse events— and the Curse, they believed would take many forms and never leave them. Deep in Ervar's mind, he was aware, the Curse, once generated by the gods, would be stealth and always present. Nevertheless, he was confident this was the right decision to take. The wooded hills had become depleted of game, land to cultivate was no longer sufficient, and the eternally dull climate, especially in winter, left the tribe little choice. Nor could Ervar dismiss the fact they were forced to be on constant alert from invasion by the slant-eyed people who lived where the sun rises. Furthermore, their cousins from where the sun never goes, were also pressing their barbaric hordes in the tribe's territory, with increasing frequency.

Visiting merchants from the countries of the internal sea had exchanged ideas with the Kaerdalh about the reliability of growing food from the soil and adventurers from the various tribes had been in the land where the sun sets by a vast ocean[1]. The climate was more clement, the land flatter and more suited for agriculture. Game was plentiful, and inhabitants spoke a similar language.

[1]Atlantic Ocean

Subsequently, the concept of migrating had matured. The decision to undertake such a vast movement was decided after many meetings between war chiefs, kings, and druids. They all spoke the same language, had the same life code, the same laws, but lived in different valleys, with minimal interaction between the various clans. Druid authority surpassed that of the tribal leaders, and had been essential to the decisions made. The associated trauma, with a move of such proportions, was huge; the travel itself was beyond the comprehension of many. No one could be left behind, all had to follow.

The spiritual implication was even more critical. Gods, in the minds of tribal members, were closely associated with the familial lands. Leaving for human reasons was not an act the divinities would empathise. Initially the druids opposed any such idea, pointing out promises of improved material well-being were shallow—if the tribes were discontent in situ, they would not be satisfied elsewhere. However, the constant incursions from warriors of other lands changed the religious cast's mind.

The Kaerdalh and neighbouring Brae met and, as previously agreed, Ervar's tribe led. Over the course of the next few days, other tribes gathered to form a huge migratory body—representing the majority of regional Celts, and all on the move. Their language was a common bond and they referred to themselves as the Bryethi nation. As far as they knew, only one other Celtic nation existed, and whose language differed slightly but belonged to the same etymological group. These people, who lived towards the direction of the midday sun, were called the Hybaer. These folks, as far as the Bryethi were aware, had not started any mass migration.

The transient Celts knew what to expect from the regions they were traversing. The journey would last roughly fifty to sixty days; the Kaerdalh and Brae had conducted many reconnaissance expeditions. They had chosen their routes carefully since they were not in a position to fight any battles while on the road; warfare had to be avoided at all cost.

Chapter Two

Ervar and his tribe, after a period of four new moons, settled on two islands in the middle of a river, surrounded by distant hills. Ervar immediately thought the mounts needed fortifying for use as a lookout and early warning system against potential incursion from possible enemies.

Four hundred families of diverse casts started to build dwellings that would later be surrounded by a defence wall; the water acting as natural protection. A system of boats to ferry people, supplies, and cattle needed creating in a second phase. Another part of the tribe settled further downstream at the foot of a big hill.

Towards where the sun never goes, was a hill taller than the others. Intriguing as it stood higher, once atop the summit, one would have a commanding view of the whole valley and a clue to what lay beyond. Ervar felt the need to investigate. On his way up, he stopped on a plateau—a clearing in the midst of an otherwise wooded area which constituted the slope leading up to the crest. From there, Ervar could see the valley below and the distant hills. He had a good feeling about the place and thought of building a hut for his own solitude. He left a marker then carried onwards.

The view from the top was appealing to a mind in need of quiet contemplation. Towards where the sun never goes, the land was flat. In the direction of the rising sun, there were two large hills, similar to the one he was standing upon. It was misty over the river and the encampment, Ervar could only guess where his tribe was at work. Where the sun sets, other hills stood proud. He had always been intrigued by that time of day... rapid changing of colours. It always inspired him with hope—he had an inexplicable urge to go towards the settling dwindling planet.

Why do we Celts always want to be where we are not? The same desire pushed us from our ancestral land. It was not so much the barbarians from the land of the sunrise, nor our cousins from the land of snow, it was that we were unsatisfied with the present and hoped for something better where the sun rests. It goes without saying our gods see our afflictions as a sin, and it is well clear in my mind, the sacrifices before our departure were not great enough to compensate them for their wrath. The future, to my mind, will be a constant battle between the guilt of leaving our motherland and the belief we upset the gods. I try to ignore them, but at the same time, I experience phases of intense fear, remorse, and superstitions.

Ervar proceeded back down to the settlement on the islands in the middle of the river. He went to see the head druid and told him about the site he had found. He suggested they see it together—a perfect place to meditate and reflect on destiny and the life of the tribe in general.

The Druid was the spiritual leader; the primary link to other tribes and the gods. The Kaerdalh was considered a "cursed" tribe as far as the other druids were concerned. Years ago, story told of a meeting between the druids and the Gods. They were discussing how every tribe showed its devotion; Ervar's tribe was falling far short of expectation. The tribe's chief at the time had no idea the gods were so disenchanted. The tribe was right to its members materialistically, but matters of creed were low in their priorities. The druids knew the state of affair but kept it a secret, transmitted only to their successors.

The current druid, Dalhman, accompanied Ervar to the hilltop, to unburden the secret of the curse. Ervar was taken aback; he felt he and his tribe had been let down by the gods and judged it a betrayal. The knowledge freed him from the constant worries of pleasing the tribe's divinities.

The current settlement was restricted by lack of land. After cogitating a few days, Ervar decided he had to find a place fitting of the tribe. He committed himself to go in search of the perfect land. He returned many times to his special place so he could watch the sunsets. His imagination ran wild as he planned his next move.

Ervar thought to follow the river on the assumption it ran into a large lake. First they needed to build a boat big enough to cope with the river, but more importantly, the vast lake and its treacherous waves and winds. They had no experience in that kind of fare. The Venete tribe, who lived in the direction where the sun sets, had a reputation for being seafarers. The origin of the Venete was nebulous, but they understood the Celtic language. They were believed to have moved away from the eastern Celtic land an age past and once at a destination, they mingled with the indigenous people, but many people still considered them Celts. Ervar believed them to be the perfect educators and hoped to recruit some of them to the Kaerdalh.

One rainy morning, in the period when the leaves fall, Ervar left his people in search of the Venete, attended by five craftsmen, twelve warriors, and Dalhman.

Fifteen nights and days went by before the Kaerdalh party reached the land of the Venete. The countryside became progressively prettier especially as they arrived at a rugged coastline with beautiful granite outcrops. Rivers cut deep into the landscape, the inlets were majestic—Ervar was in awe and developed a great admiration for the sea.

Ervar's group made contact with the Venete in the harbour of Waenn, their principal town. Their territory was on the south coast of land protruding into the ocean—Armorica, meaning land of the sea. King Walrok welcomed them, and wished them well during their stay in Waenn. He inquired about the latest migration movements in the Celtic world; probably to find out if more groups were to come.

Ervar and his men checked where the Venete built their vessels. The crafts were sturdy, tall, and a large piece of oily cloth was used to capture the wind and move the boats. They acquired the wood for building from an enchanted forest, where, they said magical spirits existed. Four boats were being built; Ervar was impressed by the Venete skill and commitment.

The Kaerdalh envoys stayed long enough to learn to build boats and how to use them. They discovered the geography of the different coastlines and seas which lay between the main continent and a substantial island in the north where the Venete used to source tin and iron.

The Venete boats were beautiful. The hulls were tall and rounded from side to side, front to back. The rear section was higher and had a platform where the tiller was. One mast was at the centre with a smaller platform at the top. The sail was rolled on an oblique piece of wood. The front had another small platform and in between was the rail for the long paddles.

Ervar found great enjoyment from their involvement with the ship-building tribe. He had to choose if they were to build ships of their own or lease part of the Venete fleet, along with their crews. Ervar decided for time's sake, expertise and cost, they would buy three ships and rent the rest. Eight hundred warriors, with their families, would total around two thousand people; one ship could take thirty passengers with luggage. Horses and various animals totalled about three hundred and finally supply vessels were required. All considered, there was a flotilla of one hundred and fifteen ships. They had to choose where the mass of the tribe would board the vessels. The Venete, who knew the coastlines of most countries, told them if they followed the river where their current settlement was; they would come to an estuary favourable for an operation of such magnitude. It implied the Celts would have to march from their present settlement to the estuary. The Venete also knew of a suitable landing site on the shore of the island, in the direction where the sun never goes.

Ervar thought too much was left to the judgment of these Venete. He decided to command an expedition with Venete navigators. They would go around the Venete coast, onto the estuary, and finally sail to the landing point on the big Island. Gold was used to pay for all the purchases and services.

A few days later they left Waenn harbour and set sail around the coast of Armorica, first in the direction of the sunset, turning then towards where the sun never sets, finally following the coastline in the direction of where the sun rises.

Ervar admired the rocky coastline, crowned mostly by woods. Thousands of small islands patched the sea, adding to the mystical feeling of the coastline. As the days progressed, they sailed by white cliffs, then sand dunes and beaches, finally reaching the estuary of the river which flowed by their camp many days up stream. Arnu, the chief of the Venete, confirmed it was the very same river. They went ashore and camped for the night.

After suitable rest and respite, all sailed onward towards the large island. The sea opened around them, and they lost the comfort of seeing land in the distance. The Kaerdalh found it strange to be in open water—it was impressive, grandiose and lonely all at the same time.

Two more days went by, land reappeared in the shape of white cliffs standing to their left. The vessels entered a natural channel leading to a river estuary; they cruised upstream and saw fields. Ervar had found his destination; he just had to go back and gather the rest of the clan.

Three months later, the bulk of the tribe was on the grassland of the new island. A payment in gold, brought all the way from the ancestral land, was used to finance the expedition and pay the Venete who delivered the flotilla on time. Soon after they arrived, the tribe determined trenches had to be built; for the first time since they left the ancestral land, they were conscious they might encounter people who would not look kindly at their arrival. The tribe expected this and had to be ready. The Kaerdalh had only eight hundred warriors, but their female folk would assist them, following the tradition that often both genders would go to battle together.

Phases of the moon came and went—an army of roughly a thousand indigenous men appeared on a hill. The situation was not favourable; the attackers were on high ground. Although they had rushed to fortify their camp, they could have done with more time; a battle strategy had to be devised at once. Ervar planned to create a diversion by moving the women and children towards the south, looking as if they were trying to escape. That action would hopefully pull some of the enemy's force toward them, and then the Celts would go up the depleted hill and outflank the attackers.

Ervar approached the tribal druid, Dalhman, to share his thoughts on the crucial battle in which they were about to engage.

'Dalhman, how will the battle prevail? Will the gods be on our side?'

'My dear Ervar, the gods have no side. Although a crucial moment for us, whatever the outcome, the gods will tell us to cope with it.'

'Can we do anything to prompt a divine intervention? Are we on our own?'

'We are the masters of our own destiny.'

'Deep down inside, I prefer it that way. It is the moment to address the troops.'

Ervar assembled the war chiefs and most of the warriors, men, and women. The custom was such that some women without children assisted their men in battle by riding with them in their chariots, supplying spears and other weapons. They were also known to charge bare-breasted, alongside their naked men, shouting war cries.

'My people, we are about to engage in a fight, our success is crucial. We have travelled all the way from our ancestral home to settle on the side of this river, on *this* island. The native inhabitants of this land consider us intruders. They will doubtless fight to defend their homeland with the same bravery we are known to have. There is no right or wrong side in this confrontation, only the will to survive. The ones with the most resolve will see the end of this day.'

No cheers were to be heard; only sullen, determined faces were on parade. Ervar climbed into his chariot, already equipped with his javelins and spare sword; his two horses stamped the ground in anticipation of the battle. He wore a shield on his left arm, laced sandals on his feet, and a plaid skirt covered his body from waist to knees. His favourite torque was around his neck, the rest of his body was bare.

The enemy started to move towards the horde of Celtic women and children, and doing so, walked down the hill in slow motion. From a distance, they resembled warriors, dressed with makeshift helmets and wooden spears.

When the enemy was nearly halfway down diagonally, Ervar gave the order to his troops. The foot soldiers were to move directly towards the descending enemy; the chariots and horsemen to the top of the hill.

Suddenly the enemy was confronted with three hordes—one manoeuvring down the river, a mass of fierce shouting soldiers running towards them, and more worrisome, a group of mounted men and chariots hurtling to the hilltop, and who met with little resistance given the token enemy forces remaining committed elsewhere. The Kaerdalh held advantage of being on the move and on the offensive. Their cavalry annihilated the enemy on the top crest of the hill. Their foot soldiers, meeting the descending foes, were slashing them open with their short glaives[2]. The Celts were more agile and more proficient in close combat. Within less than an hour, they were victorious. The triumph was such that, Wardell, head of the indigenous people, asked to see Ervar; a Venete translated Ervar's address.

'We have today defeated you. We, therefore, ask your people lay down their weapons. Half of you will follow us and help us settle on this vast island. There will be no marriages between our two groups; families will not be broken. The rest of you can return to your land.'

'These are harsh terms, and I cannot abide by them.'

'If you refuse to accept the present state of affair, there is no point in furthering our conversation.'

Ervar approached the chief, and with lightning speed, raised his sword above his head, and in an oblique downward thrust, decapitated Wardell.

[2]Glaive: Short sword with double edges.

Chapter Three

Ervar's tribe had grown from two thousand five hundred members, to dozens of thousands, eventually amassing over six hundred thousand. They left the ancestral land in roughly 600 BC; they reached Britain, "Big Island", soon after. It had taken one thousand years and thirty generations for them to reach the size they were now.

The initial settlement was in what is nowadays the city of Southampton. The Kaerdalh were never again challenged militarily following their success in the initial battle. They expanded east to what is now Kent, then west to modern Cornwall; the push towards the north did not occur until one hundred years after the landing. Little by little, they went as far north as present Cumberland, northern Yorkshire, and Northumberland. They stopped at the contemporary Scottish border, north of which dwelt a savage group of people of Celtic origin—the Scots or Hybaers. The Hybaer strain of the Celtic people left their homeland in central Europe, sojourned in Northern Spain, then sailed to Ireland, some sailed further to Alba, present day Scotland. They maintained a strained and fragile coexistence with the Picts, whose origin was, and still is, unknown. Both the Scots and especially the Picts were ferocious; their inhumane nature and ruthlessness in warfare made them redoubtable. The fact they painted they faces blue added to their daunting supernatural reputation.

The "Curse of the Rhoem", quiescent for a long time, returned in the form of the Roman invasion. Unlike their Gallic cousins, the Britons were never subjugated. Ervar's successors' uneasy cohabitation with Rome lasted nearly three hundred years. Constant fighting, but not on a great scale, took place. The Celts appropriated what they wanted out of the Roman civilisation. Dwelling and culture were, for the most part, assimilated in their day-to-day life. Their language and religion remained the same. The decline of the Roman Empire in the British Isles coincided with the push of Saxon raiders in Britain.

A descendant of Ervar, Cranadh, now reigned in a fiefdom which included the southwest of Britain. He also had sovereignty over lands in the northwest of the country near Hadrian's Wall. The year was AD 389. The kingdom was Domenea.

Cranadh was sitting to the right of Pierik, looking south to the sea. As the head druid, Pierik had the ears of his childhood friend Cranadh, the king. Their relationship had grown over thirty years.

The king was in his mid-thirties. He was of average height and his green eyes were a feature one could not miss. His lips were regular and of perfect shape; his nose was straight without being perfect. The expressions on his face betrayed his moods—annoyance was witnessed with his lower lip darting down on the left side, scepticism showed by his upper lip moving slightly upward. His body was well proportioned and exuded strength and health. Cranadh was not aware of the power of his speech; females found his singing intonations charismatic, while men were fascinated by the sound and melody of his tone more than the substance of his speech. As such, people had difficulty remembering what he said. He was frequently asked to repeat himself, and as consequence, he thought the world full of deaf and foolish individuals.

The rocky coastline was the barrier where waves came crushing. The caer or castle, stood on a bluff and had been named Finnygook, meaning fair spirit.

Cranadh and Pierik sat in the council room, observing the sheer beauty of the autumnal evening—the rocks, the sea, the waves, the green grass, the sky, the sun; all conducive to a serene and humble atmosphere, and all belonged to the spiritual life of the Domenean.

Pierik turned towards a more mundane consideration regarding Gwen, Cranadh's wife.

'Are you upset about Gwen not wanting to live with you any longer?'

'Of course, I am devastated by the situation. She was my wife, my lover, my confidant, my companion. I thought she would be in my life forever. I love her so, I had to let her go. Keeping her would have been preventing a beautiful bird from stretching its wings and exploring the air. The pain I feel stays inside me like a grey cloud that cannot be swept away, instead casting a shadow over the earth. I haven't reached the stage where I can see my part in all this tragedy. I am battered, in a state of stupor, paralysed both physically and mentally.

Aches of the heart are so painful.'

'You never saw it coming; I did. Of late, she held that faraway look when you were together. Love probably left her a while ago.'

'I sit at one of the finest views of my realm, yet I ail. That coastline is part of me, the sea is my solace, but today they are all oblivious to me. I cannot even be concerned about the hordes of Saxons putting a foot hole in the east of the island. Pierik, what do you make of these intruders?'

'I wonder whether it is an intrusion, as you put it, or a massive move on their part. These people do not come from a coastal area, they come from hilly wooded lands far away, just as our ancestors did more than a thousand years ago. The Saxons are migrating, and I believe they will not stop in the east of our isle. They are ruthless warriors and do not let anything stand in their way. Their degree of sophistication is low. They feel the need to conquer so they can assimilate our ways—there *will* be war.'

'The fiefdoms of the east are small and poorly prepared to drive back those barbarians. Do we message the lords and propose we help but risk having them interpret the gesture as hostile, or do nothing for a while and see how they cope? The latter could be dangerous—if the Saxons settle a part of the isle, however small, it will give them a stronghold. I do not trust the ability of our Celtic cousins in the east to ward off their enemy. I therefore advise all kingdoms of the east and west hold council as soon as possible; I will send messengers forthwith. Let the council meet in Sulis.'

'You're correct in your assessment of the situation. However, because your vision is so clear, you will encounter resistance from other chiefs who are not yet threatened. Not seeing the real danger the Saxons represent, will make them hesitant in order not to upset the susceptibility of the weaker members of our nation in Kent, Lundun and the northeast.'

A month later Cranadh and his entourage were on their way to Sulis. It was the most Roman city in Britain; elegance and majesty were present everywhere within its walls. Still, Cranadh's mind wandered back to Gwen. She filled the most important place in his heart. He remembered the last conversation they had together.

'My lord, my husband, I shall be leaving for Cumberland in the morning; my lady in waiting will accompany me. I would be grateful if you would grant me a strong-armed escort to go back to my family's estate near Carwick.'

'Gwen, my life companion, I am mortified you feel the need to leave me. You are more important to me than my realm, and yet the realm has been the very reason for not having enough time or courage to tell you what you mean to me, and how much I want to please you. My intention to do right by you was always there, but perversely, I still found an excuse not to follow through. I was inattentive. Behind my mask of serenity, you should know there is a boiling heart—a passionate lover. You must remember our embraces were the result of two people deeply in love with each other.'

'My Lord, what you have said is a speech hollow to my ears. Words come naturally to you, but your actions prove you to be self-seeking, in pursuit of governing the kingdom. I needed to participate, which you never offered. I was not to be your queen, only a lover, and that could only take us so far.'

'I have not kept you informed of the affairs of the realm, not because I thought you incapable, but I wanted to spare you from the drudgeries of running a state. I realise, now, I was wrong to treat you in such a fashion.'

'My husband, my king, I have become conscious I cannot be your partner on several matters; I cannot be *King Cranadh's* wife. I owe it to you and myself to act truthfully, and we must part.'

A long silence fell... both realised everything was over.

'Do you want the Cumbrian Guard to escort you?'

'Yes, of course, my Lord.'

Chapter Four

The council of the Celtic kingdoms of Britain took place in the former Roman governor's palace; the occupants had left a few years ago. The building was an enormous structure, in the heart of Sulis. Among well-tailored gardens, it portrayed the typical splendour of Roman architecture: columns, interior courts, basins, mosaic, waterworks, huge pools, and rooms with steps.

The meeting convened in an indoor auditorium. A majestic circular table was at the centre of it—it seated sixteen. Today, eleven were present.

The kings, chief of tribes and fiefdoms wore Celtic attire. Ordinarily, they dressed in Roman garb, but for a meeting of the council, they adorned the costume of their ancestors. It consisted of a plaid garment around their waist, a leather plastron over their chest, and a winged helmet. On their left side hung a flat and broad sword, wrist guards with patterns and that most personal of jewellery, the torque. The shape and motifs on each torque went a long way to identify one's status; it was circular in appearance with a gap at the front of the neck.

The torque, made of gold, bronze or iron, was a permanent ornament, and the pattern intricacies reflected the bearers standing in society.

Eleven councilmen sat in a circle around the table:
- Hervey of Kent; his realm included Kent and the southern estuary of the Tamesas.
- Yan of Lundun.
- Pierig; his domain formed an area north of the Tamesas and the Marshes.
- Allan; his fiefdom incorporated the south of Lundun to the sea.
- Ewen; all the land north of Lundun up to the borderland with the Picts and Scots, including the east coastline to the Oceanus Germanicus.
- Merrill; west of the Penniorcoches.
- Morgan; Cymru.
- Hywell; East Cymru and Borderland.
- Malosh; Cricklade and Gwent.
- Cranadh; Kernow, Dumnonia, Dorsetshire and all the land up to the estuary of the Sabrina. Cumberland was also under his administration. It was the richest due to the tin mining and the commerce of taking place with the continent, south of Britain.

Cranadh and Ewen possessed the most substantial of the military forces.

Brennan, the most prominent druid in all of Britain, and living at the court of Hervey of Kent, pronounced an invocation. 'All of you around this table are blessed to guide our Celtic people in this beloved island. Our ancestors landed on these shores many years ago. At that time, we were a small tribe; we brought the cult of the gods who guide us and whom we still worship. During the council, you must be true to our past and remain humble in front of our deities—listen to their voices through your own conscience.' Brennan did not mention that understandings of the paths leading to communications with the gods were different for every participant.

Advisors and confidants backed each person sitting at the table. Nearly one hundred people filled the auditorium.

Ewen led the assembly. 'Brothers! We stand here today to evaluate the situation created by the landing of these Saxon hordes. We will listen to our comrades from the frontline then have a forum to see what we can do. We must respect one another and exchange words in a civilised manner. Hervey, would you care to tell the assembly about the state of affairs in Kent?'

Hervey of Kent took the floor. 'It is true several landings by Saxon troops have occurred in the last three months. They have destroyed some coastal villages, and there has been loss of life. They have not, so far, expanded further. We have observed them and estimate the three landing sites hold about three thousand men.'

Ewen noticed another member of the council looking to contribute. 'Morgan, do you wish to speak?'

Morgan's accent was difficult to understand, however Hywell, the other Welshman had no problem with it.

'I do, Ewen. I want to ask our brother Hervey his reason for not engaging with these barbarians. Is he waiting for additional immigrant enemies to land so he can kill more at once? Notice I used the words "immigrant enemies" because there is no doubt in my mind these people did not land with the goal of pillaging a few of our villages... they are the spearhead of something bigger to come.'

Hervey was quick to respond. 'Ewen, Morgan, kings, chieftains, my brother Celts. In my realm, we view the landing of the Saxons with worried eyes. We observe, scrutinise their moves, and contain their expansion. We do not feel it necessary to overwhelm them. Their number, as far as we can estimate is about three thousand. If it were to reach five thousand, there would be cause to review the situation. Every effort to enter into a dialogue has so far been fruitless. Life, in general, has not changed in my territory, and frankly, after the initial shock and loss of lives, which numbered one hundred and fifty, nothing has happened since.'

Ewan invited Cranadh to speak.

Cranadh got up and heaved a sigh. He was calm but forceful in his bearing. 'Our brother Hervey has the unenviable experience of facing circumstances he did not wish for, but we realise what is happening in his kingdom concerns all of us. We share the same bloodline as the Kentish people. We also recognise their plight today will be ours tomorrow, and I therefore propose each realm send troops to Kent to help Hervey rid his lands of the Saxons. A strong message has to be delivered to the invaders. A mighty blow has to be stricken; a blow so strong it will annihilate these barbarians. None must survive, bar one, who will carry the news back to their homeland—the Celts are *not* to be tampered with.'

Yann of Lundun chose this juncture to voice his opinion. 'It could have the opposite effect and make them wild, giving them reason to invade in much higher numbers.'

Cranadh was resolute. 'We must be prepared to kill more if they dare to try.'

Hervey of Kent dared to show resistance towards Cranadh. 'Let me make myself clear on the subject of any of your troops marching into my territory. It will *not* happen. Your military presence in Kent will have a devastating effect on my people. You know full well, it is tough to restrain any armed warriors to behave themselves. Thieveries, rapes, disturbances, all would be widespread, and my conscience refuses to impose all this on my people. You have to trust me to find the right decision and get rid of the Saxons in my own time, in my own way.'

Merrill intervened. 'Cranadh rightly foresees that what is now an incursion, will develop into a full-scale invasion by tribes who envy the way we live and covet our land. Hervey! It is unfortunate they landed in your realm, but the problem is not yours alone. I doubt you can contain this hostile threat, and if you are over-powered, then all of us are in danger. We need to help you and at the same time help ourselves.'

'I will not allow any of you to march your troops all over my land. I am greatly insulted and do not feel there is any point staying here any longer.'

The council ended with that statement. The advocates of sending troops into Kent could not force themselves to act and be unwelcome. Factions appeared. Hervey of Kent, Yan of Lundun, Pierig of the Marshes, and Allan of the South stood for non-aggression and a wait and see policy. The realms of the West, North, Cymru and Cymru borderland were for pushing back the invaders immediately but did not want to appear as conquerors of other Celtic kingdoms.

Cranadh was melancholic on the journey back—Gwen was leaving him, and the possible loss of Celtic lands in the east added up to his seeing life on the bleak side. He wondered if he ought to be more forceful in trying to defend the heritage of the past. His conscience said yes. He thought the present Celts were the guardians of the values and history of all generations who had come before them. They had no right to let themselves be taken over by barbarians. They had resisted the Romans and did not submit to them, but took what they thought was appropriate. The Saxons meant trouble; their warriors fought well and were fierce in battle. The "Curse of the Rhoem" would inevitably surface from the dark past. Cranadh was compelled to take action—every ancestor was looking at him, his lineage occupied a prevalent place in his conscience. Ervar, his legendary ancestor, the one who led his people from the deep heart of Europe to Britain, was a constant companion to Cranadh's mind. He felt overwhelmed, but at the same time accountable for his race, the gods, and for what the Celtic world stood for. *Would it be out of line to invade Kent? No, not if it was good for the rest of Britain.*

Britain was directly named for the groups of tribes called the Bryethi who were part of the first migration.

Chapter Five

The council had ended on a mixed note; there were no guarantees the eastern kingdoms would stop the incursions.

Cranadh reached Finnygook and isolated himself in his chambers; he was physically exhausted. The curse, the situation with the Saxons, and the attitudes of the chiefs of the East, were problems without answers or solutions. His mental exhaustion took over, and he sank into a deep melancholy. Gwen was at the centre of his emotions; his feelings towards her burned his heart. She had left, and Cranadh felt consumed by loneliness knowing she was not nearby. Depression settled in and added to his general fatigue—he fell into a deep sleep.

Cranadh found himself transported through the sky at terrific speed, whisking through clouds and finally coming to rest in front of three figures. All had long white beards, long hair and wore white robes. He recognised them to be Teuta—God of all Celts, Taran—God of War and Llew—God of Omnipotence. Cranadh thought he was going to be drowned and sacrificed to Teuta, burned and offered to Taran, or hanged and given to Llew. He wondered if he was in another life. Among Celts, death was not a finite event, it was just a step into another life. Teuta spoke to him and put an end to his questions.

'Cranadh, do you think you are an excellent Celt?'

Cranadh, horrified by the question, endeavoured to answer humbly. 'I have tried to be, with various degrees of success. Teuta, spiritual chief to all of us, you know what I have done, and I can only refer to your judgment for my answer.'

'You are right, I know every single act of your lifetime. From here on, I will pose questions to which I know the answers. I want you to hear yourself articulate the responses, so *you* become aware of what you have done in your life. Have you done everything you could to live by the law of the gods?'

'I have acted to the best of my conscience, hoping it followed our spiritual laws. On many occasions, I have behaved as my conscience dictated. I have also acted out of fear, and it has led me to selfish acts. As chief of a tribe, I have served as a representative of my cast should act but have considered the effects it could have on the less fortunate.'

'My dear Cranadh, we know how much dilemma goes into your thinking. We know the constant fray in your conscience between your heart and your duties, between your compassion and your prejudgments, between your weaknesses and your strengths. Cranadh, you are a permanent battlefield. There is something else we want to ask you... do you know why we, the gods, exist?'

Cranadh felt like a child questioned by his teacher.

'Well, you exist because you are keepers of the virtues of our race. You live to guide us, support us, you exist to defend us, you exist because you are the guardians of infinite knowledge, you exist because you created earth, water, fire, ether, life, everything which we love and revere. You support our institutions, our hierarchy.'

'We are keepers of virtues but not of your race alone. We guide and support you, and everybody else. We are custodians of universal knowledge. We are aware of your institutions and rules, but we are in no way their keepers. We are the universal energy, intuition, and goodness present in concrete and abstract matters. Every living being in the universe has our awareness. We are myths, we are bonds, we are the fruits of all human beings' imaginations, hopes, feelings, and thoughts. We are anything to everything... everything to anything. We are some of what you want us to be, but also we are not what you want us to be. We have no vanity, no pride. We are esoteric and realistic. We are not of your universe; we are of a realm you cannot begin to perceive. We love you as we love anybody and anything. We are not yours alone.'

Cranadh was stunned. He was bewildered and shocked; the long-lasting veneration he had for the gods all his life was nothing but fiction. He thought the gods had no loyalty to him and the Celtic people; the idea they existed for everybody was inconceivable. Cranadh felt betrayed. The gods should have told them years ago that they, the Celts, were not the chosen people.

Cranadh spoke to Llew, God of Omnipotence. 'Llew, why didn't you tell us we are nothing special to you? So many beliefs and rules exist because we thought we were your first brood.'

'Cranadh, many generations of your ancestors used us to make a full legend and interpretation of what we are. We are the essence and spiritual power of many things. We are the synergy of many creatures and happenings, *but* we do not belong to, nor favour any specific ideals or beings. From their imagination, your ancestors created a relationship to us that does not exist. They used us for their earthly needs without asking for our opinions.'

'Well, you could have told them where you stood.'

'We do not behave that way—we let things happen in their own time. We are gods of the Romans, Saxons, and the Hybaers. Our spirit is universal, and we do not take sides. We do not quarrel amongst ourselves, and when you engage one of us, you address us all.'

Taran became no longer the silent observer. 'The destiny of the Celts is a long one. The Saxons will conquer all Big Island, and you will be pushed west into Kernow and Cymru. The Hybaers, which include the Irish and Scots, will stay free for an extended period but will eventually become subdued. In Gaul, their Celtic blood will mix with Germanic, and all over Europe, people will not even know they were of Celtic origin. The descendants of the Saxons, as the Hybaer will call them, will treat the Irish with particular disdain. Cranadh! Your tribe will go across the sea to Armorica and build a kingdom over there.'

Cranadh gasped at such a prospect.

Taran proceeded to be the bearer of bad tidings. 'Dark years and centuries will fall upon all of you. Terrible things will happen. Celts, serving different masters, will fight Celts. They will forget they were ever brothers. As a result of their bravery, they will serve as warriors, working for causes which have nothing to do with their spiritual interests. They will pay dearly with their blood for supporting unworthy ideas. In the more distant future, they will be sent as settlers to faraway lands, and only then, will they start to emerge from that bleak period. After many thousand moons, there will be a multitude of great Celtic individuals who realise their blood survived all these years. Their ancestral consciousness will resurface, craving for their cultures and ancient beliefs; their lament will be in having lost so much. They will become fatalistic during those dark years and believe a curse was upon them. There is not, and never will be a curse on your people—only a self-fulfilling prophecy. Fear of the supernatural will make you superstitious, and always ready to throw yourselves into religious activities. Your religions will stand you apart from other people on earth—you will use it to differentiate yourselves, to console, to keep your hopes, and you will identify with them. You will believe in different forms of faith and will fight each other in the bitterest of ways because of it. I shudder to think about these conflicts. And yet, you will be one of the most educated nations on this planet and carry an artistic strain in your veins, creating such beauty in the form of poetry, music, jewellery, and writing.'

Cranadh knelt, his arms opened, his mouth gaping, his eyes round with amazement. It was a lot for him to assimilate, and he was not sure he could understand what he had heard.

'So we are not privileged, you don't care about us any more than you care about those wretched Saxons. All my ancestors were mistaken. They were led to believe we were your people. I cannot comprehend your words; it sounds like you were mocking us, and pretending all these centuries. You want me to go back to my fellow Celts and

tell them you don't care about them. I cannot do that!
Cranadh opened one eye then the other. The room was dark; the wind from the sea moved the velvet curtains. He was sweating heavily. He had had a vision while asleep, so terrifying, it was an effort trying to assemble the disjointed pieces in his head. Slowly, he reconstructed his thoughts. *How could the gods not be there for their chosen family?* He put everything in the deep closet of nightmares, and would not mention anything to anybody.

Cranadh felt lost, maybe because he was helpless, his thoughts drifted to his mother, Annick; she was the daughter of a Celtic chief from Armorica. During her youth, she had known wars and constant battles with the Romans. She was from the northern part of Armorica; the tribe she was born into never accepted the Roman occupation. For more than three hundred years, it had been a constant battle with an occupier Hell-bent on imposing their language, and institutions. Annick's tribe only adopted the way to dress and mode of habitation of the invader; as for religion, writing, and traditions, they remained the same as they had been for centuries. Her people had paid a high price, and their quality of life had severely been affected.

Annick's experience had made her a robust introverted person with extreme pride of her heritage. For Cranadh, she represented the old ways. He knew she had endured a lot in her younger days. He had listened many times to her stories, and anecdotes; they had created an image of his mother, which was respectful and powerful, a real anchor and stabilising influence. One of her favourite tales he cherished, was when she was eight years old, during a raid by a small Roman cohort, her beloved pet dog was injured by a Roman spear through one of his back legs. She nursed it to recovery until he could run like a young pup.

Annick used to tell him, 'You see, Cranadh, my dog was a Celt. He could be wounded, but he eventually came back to the fore.'

His mother was a harsh person, not affectionate, but dedicated to her son. Her relation to Cranadh's father was intense. It was her duty to be a loyal wife in every aspect, but she was always ready to criticise him, and in some ways, he was afraid of her. She respected his status as a king, however, when it came to more prosaic matters, she was not timid in voicing her opinions. They were not of the same strata in Celtic nobility; he was a blue blood of the utmost refined lineage, in contrast, she was from a small tribe that had to fight to avoid obliteration by the Romans. Her ethics and looks made her as royal as her spouse.

Cranadh was always wary of his mother; she had a quick temper and was difficult to please. His father, Ropaz, was deceased. When alive, although not demonstrative, he was kind and exuded love, even without saying a word. Cranadh had loved his father; he had been a quiet man with a powerful charisma. Cranadh had never known his grandparents.

The day following his vision, Cranadh met with Fanch, the chancellor of the realm. Fanch was an old friend of Ropaz; well versed in politics of the kingdom, and family affairs of Cranadh's relatives. They talked about the meeting in Sulis. Both decided it had amplified the difference between the eastern tribes on one side, and the northern and western ones on the other. Fanch and Cranadh agreed they should rapidly inspect the kingdom's state of readiness for war.

The equipment, the men, the horses, the supplies... all had to be surveyed, and there was no better man than Poher of Dugoat with which to confer.

Poher was the army commander in chief. He had been looking for a respectable war since birth. A conventional war was killing barbarians, but Romans, Picts, Scots or Irish would have satisfied him equally.

Cranadh's realm was called Domenea It consisted of what are now Dorset, Devon, Somerset, Cornwall, Shropshire, and Gloucestershire. Standing separately, Cumbria (Lake District) also belonged to the realm.

Roughly four hundred thousand people lived in the kingdom. The armed forces were ten thousand army and three thousand navy strong; three-quarters of them were in Domenea and the rest in the north.

The navy anchored in what are now Weymouth, Plymouth, Bristol, and Whitehaven in Cumbria with a fleet of around one hundred and fifty ships. They had three duties; marine warfare, transporting troops and shipping supplies.

The army had several functions, one of them was to act as border patrols, and another to subdue unrest and disorder. They were used to stop tribal feuds, prevent incursions from foreign tribes, remaining Roman patrols, Viking landings, Irish pirates, and perform internal policing in general. They were stationed in garrison towns and in outposts at the borders in the north.

The military had to be ready to move fast at a moment's notice; cavalry was the dominant weapon. Chariots were also used for frontal attacks and transportation; they were light and could be dismantled with ease so men could carry them over rough terrain. The unit was a squadron and numbered three hundred men—two hundred and twenty-five mounted and seventy-five chariots drivers. Foot soldiers were used on special occasions when the enemy force was dominant, and a sustained battle had to be fought. The unit for foot soldiers was a cohort, five hundred-strong. It consisted of three hundred foot soldiers, fifty projectile specialists, one hundred mounted soldiers, and fifty chariots drivers.

Cranadh asked Pierik to join him and Fanch, to have a debate with Poher about the type of military actions likely to take place if Saxons invaded the east of Britain. They wanted to identify the form of engagements of such a threat, and the implications for updating the army.

The navy had to be increased; to patrol and have an ability to move troops quickly was essential. For that purpose, flat keelboats with oars and sails had to be built. Such ships had to be ready to go ashore anywhere and land troops, as well as being able to destroy the enemy's craft by sinking them. Ships with the capability of throwing projectiles also had to be increased. Roman tactics were to be studied and adapted to that type of warfare. The four concluded their foot soldier units needed to expand and be equipped with spears and bows. If the landing of the Saxons could not be prevented, it was presumed full-fledged battles would prevail instead of "hit and run" skirmishing.

≈≈≈

The Celtic world was now in a state of flux. The Romans had occupied Gaul for nearly four centuries. The Gauls spoke a Latin language and had adopted Roman science and administration. The religion, however, was a mixture of Christianity and druidic beliefs. Their legal system was still full of the old Celtic laws.

The Hybaer lived in two different locations. Part of them had emigrated to Alba and called themselves Scots. The majority had stayed in what is present day Ireland and had never been invaded; as a result, they were living in a different manner, which was closer to the old ways. Their economy was under-developed and they practiced raiding Britain on a regular basis for booty and slaves.

The Scots and ancestral dwellers of Alba, namely the Picts, were even more cut off from the mainstream; they were fierce, and inspired terror on any population with which they came in contact. They had never been subjugated.

Cranadh's world was peaceful, momentarily, but it was easy to see many threats were taking shape on the horizon and he sensed changes were about to take place. Preparing his armed forces for new circumstances was a sensible approach.

In less than a year the transformation had been achieved, and the rejuvenation of the armed forces was a reality.

Chapter Six

It was that time of year when the days which had decreased in length started getting longer again. The Christians had chosen that occasion to commemorate the birthday of their God's son. During the same period, the druids celebrated in thanks to the gods for darkness losing over light, and the victory of hope over fear. For both sides, it was a time filled with joy and festivities.

Cranadh was looking at the solstice period with nostalgia. It was a time for reunion with family and friends. The king of Kernow, one of his titles, did not have many relatives. His mother was alive, but his father had passed away. He had uncles and aunts from the maternal and paternal sides of his family, but they were not in close vicinity of the palace. His cousins on both sides were quite dear to him, but he did not see them very often. His late uncle Brennus was the younger brother of his father; he had a son called Gralon who would become regent if Cranadh happened to die without heir or a successor too young to govern. Gralon lived in the extremity of Kernow and was keen on seafaring. Cranadh had given him a commission in his navy giving him charge of a fleet squadron. Gralon had not been groomed to become king, and that concerned Cranadh but he had not done anything to start the process either.

Cranadh's thoughts drifted back to the fact he was spending the festivities as a bachelor. Gwen, his queen, would not be present. They did not have any children, and inside his heart, Cranadh blamed Gwen for it—the demon of infertility cursed her. If Cranadh had been honest, he would have admitted her infertility suited him for a while. He sought spiritual solace from his friend Efflam.

Efflam was an Irish priest who had the ears of Cranadh. He was a typical product of the Celtic Christian Church. Most of Ireland, Cymru, and Kernow were territories, which had espoused Christianity but in a different way from the dominant strain followed by Rome. The Roman Church was heir to the doctrine of St. Paul, who single-handedly, deformed the gospel of Jesus in order to create a church full of fears for its practitioners. On the other hand, the Celtic Church had for hereditary, the Nazarene movement which had transmitted the teaching of Jesus in its purest form, via Egypt then spread to Britain and eventually Ireland. This strain of Christianity did not believe in the original sin and deemed Jesus to be a mortal who preached a doctrine based on love and non-aggression. It was strange the relationship and contact with the people from Ireland was either violent because of the raiding parties landing in Britain, or spiritual due to the influence of Irish monks and priests. The peculiar fact was Ireland had only started conversion to Christianity by Briton's missionaries. The young Irish Church, in turn, produced a brand of religious men who felt compelled to spread the way *they* saw Christianity. It was more ascetic and still impregnated by the old traditions.

Cranadh started thinking about his family and his place in history. He was well aware of his lineage—part of his education had taught him the far-reaching stories of the tribe traveling from a land, now central Europe, to Gaul then on to Britain. He sensed it was up to him to steer his people on a path that would not offend his ancestors. He was the keeper of the values of the tribe—he was responsible for its future. He knew, deep inside, he could not let his nation disappear from the face of this planet. The Saxon threat was going to be a real test to his resolve. He turned towards Efflam, to confer with the priest. He felt a discussion on a higher spiritual level would shake him from his downhearted mood.

'Efflam, my dear fellow, why does God let people of my rank govern others?'

'Your Excellency, the humblest of your subjects is your equal in the eyes of God. The poorest subject of your tribe or kingdom, in carrying out his daily duties, is as important as you are. He is part of the whole universe just as much as you are. My king, you can take actions which affect a lot of people, and that is a responsibility bestowed upon you. If you are resolute, it is an honour as well as a duty which you cannot take lightly. God knows all this, and he does not consider you more privileged than the humblest of the humblest.'

'You know I am baptised, but I am superstitious, or shall I say the old spiritual druidic beliefs influence me. My ancestors, and to some extent myself, think we are predestined to lead others.'

'The main difference between the Druidic way and Christianity is the fact druids see the Gods as an extension of humankind and will therefore impart earthly considerations and human values. God, and his son Jesus are above all that. God sees you as a person who has a responsibility to take action for others, the druids see you as a privileged being. I respect the mission that is yours, and I feel compassion for you, because of the difficulties that go with it.'

'I hear you, Efflam, do I agree with you? Probably not. As an aside, what do you think about the Saxon peril?'

'We know this island is the envy of many from across the sea, from the Vikings to the Irish, and other barbaric Teutonic tribes. It also divides us on how to face them. If they are permitted to land in any strength, it will be a significant challenge to the way we live; it brings us a time of reckoning and potentially centuries of isolation. Saxons are not coming here to befriend us, they come to conquer, take what is valuable from us, leave what is worthless, and destroy the rest. They are after our land rather than our culture. Hundreds of years ago, we moved from our ancestral grounds for fear of aliens coming to take what we had; I am afraid we are in the same situation. If we do not kill this syndrome in its infancy, it will take us over. As a man of the cloth I should be more tolerant towards these Saxons, but I feel they bring a danger to our Christian way.'

'I agree. It is inevitable we are heading for a conflict with these barbarians. I am seriously considering confrontation with the Saxons and throwing them back to the sea. It probably means I will upset some of my brethren from the east. Their inaction is incomprehensible to me, they agonise over the landing of these Saxons, and act as though paralysed with fear.'

'Fears and inactions from the eastern fiefdoms play into the Saxons' hands.'

Chapter Seven

Time for action had finally arrived. The Domenean army was on the move, en route for the east of Britain, the Kentish realm was the destination.

Cranadh was riding his horse at the canter to meet a scouting party coming back from patrol. They had been trying to make sure the rest of the army was not going to meet any armed band of the Kentish Celtic tribe They had been on the move for about a week, crossing other tribes' territories, and so far, not one had interfered with their march eastwards.

Twelve squadrons of cavalry with three hundred men each were on the go, including two thousand seven hundred horsemen and nine hundred chariots. Two cohorts were on board ships which sailed from Plymouth a week earlier. The forces transported by sea comprised six hundred foot soldiers, one hundred projectile specialists with their equipment, two hundred mounted soldiers, and one hundred chariots. The fleet was twenty ships-strong for transportation of the troops, and another twenty units for escorting and destroying enemy vessels.

The plan was to encircle the Saxon strongholds near the shore and land the seafaring troops at strategic locations to prevent the Saxons from running away. The Teuton main camp was in Mordon.

Cranadh was waiting for another envoy to report on the position of the fleet. In the meantime, he was also keeping an eye out for Hervey, the chief of the Kentish tribe, who had vowed at the Sulis council never to let troops from other tribes on his land. Cranadh had anticipated Hervey, who had a small army, would do nothing, at least for the time being.

At last, the messenger arrived, bringing news the fleet was ten miles east of Mordon, near the coast. Cranadh and Poher, his army chief, decided to move into position under cover of the night, and attack the Saxons in the thick of darkness at a set moment. At the same time, the fleet would land the foot soldiers and destroy as many enemy vessels as possible.

It was March; the moon was in its first quarter. The enemy camp was a half-mile across with a wide opening beachside. Their defensive structures were minimal. Cranadh's cavalry was about quarter of a mile away from the Saxon encampment. The Domenean forces had moved close without raising the alarm among the Saxons. The fleet had sailed near the shore under cover of darkness, and small boats had already landed troops on the coast next to the camp. The rest were waiting to disembark once the mounted troops commenced their charge. A flaming arrow shot to the heavens was the signal for the soldiers in the ships to spring into action.

The cavalry started at a trot, accelerated to a canter, and then to a gallop. The instructions were not to yell at the mounted soldiers advancing towards Saxon positions. When they finally reached the encampment, all Hell broke loose. The flaming arrow went up. The surprise was total. The Saxons' were caught unaware; few were running around, most were still asleep. Their dwelling canvases were set on fire, Celtic horsemen were entering tents, and every occupant was speared, beheaded or disembowelled. The few barbarians trying to escape towards the beach, met with landed troops, rounded up like cattle and taken prisoners.

It was a belief among the Celts the spirit of a person resided in one's head, so it was imperative in combat to behead one's enemy. That way, you took not only his life but also his soul. It was essential to humiliate these intruders.

Within a couple of hours, one thousand Saxons lay dead, and the rest were prisoners. By the time the sun came up, all Saxons still standing were herded; around two thousand of them.

Radnor, the chief of the vanquished, stood there, weaponless, looking proud and arrogant in defeat. Poher approached him, and with one mighty blow decapitated the Saxon leader. A noise of general astonishment rose from the enemy's ranks.

Cranadh and Poher had decided to exterminate the rest of the defeated invaders—the plan was to put as many of the Saxons in their boats, tow them to the high sea and when ten miles from the shore, set the vessels on fire and sink them. The rest were to be tied up and killed by sword, spears, and arrows. They were divided into twenty groups and systematically murdered. When the rest of the Saxons, caught wind of what was going to happen to them they tried to escape, but the cavalry marshalled them back. The noise made by these wretched people was unreal. It was a vision of Hell. It took a volley of arrows to contain them, spears and swords did the rest. There were streams of blood, and the stench from the bodies killed during the night started to reek.

The carnage was finished by sundown. A small group had been spared, with the purpose of letting them return to their homeland, and relate to their own kind what had happened to them.

The armed forces from Domenea had very few casualties and even fewer fatalities. It was a great victory; although it is said in any conflict even the victor loses something. The Celts of Domenea had lost a part of their souls in that day of bloodshed; this date would live to be a time for the possible rekindling of the "Curse of the Rhoem".

Cranadh and Poher decided to leave the following morning. In the meantime, an entrenched camp was built in readiness should the forces of Hervey of Kent choose to pay them a visit.

At first light, a row of mounted men from the kingdom of Kent stood in line; their number close to a thousand.

Hervey, King of Kent; next to him a horseman carrying the standard, a rampant white horse on a red background. They trotted towards the Domenean camp. Hervey shouted to see Cranadh. Cranadh and Poher emerged from the entrenched camp carrying the flag of Kernow, black with a white cross.

'Cranadh, you are intruding on my realm, it was none of your business to attack these Saxons. I had concluded an agreement with them to let them in peace as long as they stayed in their camp. Now the accord has been broken by your reckless act, they will come back in increasing numbers.'

'After hearing what you have just told me, it reinforces my views you are a weak man with short vision, and a traitor to the cause of the Brythonic Celtic nations at large. What I did yesterday will send a message back to the Saxons they cannot be safe if they land on our island. What you fail to understand, Hervey, is your agreement was endangering every Celt on this island of ours. These Saxons only understand violence.'

'The Saxons will not forget, and like the Romans, they will carry their grudge for years and years, just as Julius Caesar avenged the sack of Rome by the Celts, which had occurred hundreds of years before he conquered Gaul.'

'I do not wish to confer with you any longer. I will leave this camp today and will be out of your territory within two days. We are only passing, but if you decide to attack us, we will kill every single one of your men of arms. We have no quarrel with you.'

As Cranadh articulated these words, he saw Hervey as a traitor, a fool, and a coward. He had to get rid of him now. He rode away from the king of Kent and conferred with Poher, still riding at his side.

'Poher, I am going to kill that weakling, and I am going to kill him now. Ride back to our troops, and by the time your reach our line, Hervey's head will be rolling in the grass. Sound the alarm and move towards Hervey's men, we will carry out battle with them. I am going to kill him before he goes to the Saxons to ask for their protection.'

Poher's mouth was agape. 'Cranadh, I think it is rather extreme. By the same token, I believe action ten times superior to negotiation.'

'Leave me the standard.'

Poher rode back towards his line of soldiers while Cranadh trotted towards Hervey. On nearing the Kentish king, he prodded him in the stomach with the Kernow standard then dropped it. Surprised and out of breath, Hervey bent forward. Cranadh drew his sword and, in an upward thrust decapitated the king. The Kent flag carrier, taken by shock, seemingly made for his sword, but before he could reach it, a blow from Cranadh struck him across his chest, and he galloped away like a dismembered puppet.

Poher led a charge with the totality of the cavalry against a fleeing Kentish force, which had been stunned by the beheading of their king. Hervey's men of arms had no intention of putting up any type of stand, only a few decided to turn back and fight.

Cranadh was satisfied—he had pushed the Saxons back to the sea and killed a coward king. He had no intention to stay in Kent any longer than necessary.

Within three days Cranadh was back in Domenea. Other British Celtic kingdoms might feel dejected, but he was not going to be apologetic... it was time for him to think about his next move.

Chapter Eight

Having momentarily settled the Saxon problem, dealing with the Irish raiders was long overdue. For decades, they had landed in Domenea, and taken all kinds of booty, they had also been known to kidnap people for use as slaves. Cranadh thought it was time to deal with these incursions, and bring about a final solution. Besides, he owed it to his subjects to protect them from being attacked by Irish pirates. Tactically, he had to defend his rear so he could fully concentrate on the Saxons whenever the threat resurfaced.

An expeditionary force of vast size was organised, including an assembled fleet thirty ships-strong. It was common knowledge most of the Irish raiders were from the west of Erin. It was populated by poor farmers who had converted to piracy and raiding to supplement their wretched existence.

The expedition left in the spring. The fleet rounded the southwest headlands of Erin then sailed northeast across the estuary of a big river; Shannon. The bay of Lahinch was the objective of their expedition; the journey had taken ten days of rough sailing.

The Domenean army anchored in the inlet and landed a force of eight hundred men on shore. Seven hundred moved inland, one hundred stayed near the beach to fortify the landing site, the rest stayed on board to prevent an eventual attack from the sea. Their presence was seemingly undetected, however they had not doubt it would not be the case for long.

Due to the humidity coming from the ocean, Erin was beautifully green. The inhabitants were distant cousins of the Celts from Britain. Legend had it they had come from the same ancestral lands in central Europe. Instead of settling in Gaul, they had carried on to the Iberian Peninsula, and from there sailed to Erin. They had met little resistance from the original dwellers. The Irish had evolved in a different way from the Britons; the Roman influence had not reached them, so they had remained close to the old ways in every aspect of their life. Christianity had little impact on Irish society. Economically, they were behind the Britons. Their language, although of the same linguistic root, was incomprehensible to a Briton, as they spoke the Hybaer variety of the Celtic tongue.

With the landing completed, the troops chosen to go to the interior started moving towards a town called Ennistimon. They reached the outskirts early afternoon. The news of their landing travelled faster than they could move, and there was quite a crowd lined up to see them. They were watched since they had gone ashore. Cranadh and Poher were not worried; they knew there was little organised force in that part of the island.

Ennistimon was more an agglomeration of huts than a town. There were no churches or official buildings. A green knoll stood in the centre. Standing atop was a bald-headed old man with a white beard, dressed in grey, with a brown wrap across his chest and shoulders; his pants were hanging above his bare feet. Cranadh and Poher reached the green, surrounded by their soldiers. The inhabitants were standing away from the mass of Britons. Efflam stood next to the chiefs of the Britons. The old man, Seamus, was the patriarch of the district. Efflam spoke Irish so a meeting was convened outside the cluster, in the open space. The Britons put up a tent, and the conference was underway. The two Britons, Cranadh, Poher, and Efflam the Irish born, were present, on the Irish side, Seamus, and two of his councilmen attended.

The Celts from Domenea stated they had no more tolerance for raiders coming from this part of the world and issued an ultimatum. The slaves taken in captivity had to be freed within one day; a cartload of stolen properties, and artefacts from pillaged churches and monasteries had to be returned within two days; all the pirate's ships were to be destroyed. Failure to comply would result in the burning down of Ennistimon. The Irish agreed to everything except returning stolen properties, which they claimed, had been dispersed throughout Ireland. The Domeneans remained steadfast in their threat to burn Ennistimon to the ground. The Irish retorted it was materially impossible to give back the loot, and instead Seamus offered his granddaughter Bridgit, as a gesture of his willingness to cooperate. Cranadh was surprised by the guarantee and immediately suspected foul play—the Irish were known to be canny, and would use any mean to suit.

Seamus' goals were to get rid of the Britons as soon as possible, keep most of the loot, preserve the fleet intact, and deliver as few slaves as credibly believable. Against all the demands, the loss of one granddaughter was a small price to pay. Cranadh ordered his men of arms to move closer to him.

'Seamus, venerable fellow, I am entirely taken back by your offer, but I cannot accept such a young creature to be used in this fashion instead the hostage will be you. If, by tomorrow sundown, you have not delivered ten chariots of loot and released one hundred slaves, you will die with your chieftains, here present. I shall retire to the outskirts of your village, and you and your council shall accompany. I have no doubt you have sent envoys to neighbouring tribes to come to your rescue... we are prepared for such an eventuality. Come Seamus!'

The elder did not say a word; he was outguessed.

'Come to think of it, Bridgit will accompany us too.'

A small camp had been erected outside the Irish community where Seamus and his clan heads were taken in custody. Cranadh had Bridgit brought to his tent. She walked into the Briton's quarters; she did not appear afraid, upset or shocked. Bridgit was of medium build and strikingly beautiful. Her shoulders were squared but not too broad, her waist showed a gentle curvature, her legs, which one could guess through the length of her skirt, were long enough to give a sense of balance to the rest of her body. Her breasts were shapely and presumably firm without being big. Her face was angelic with rosy cheeks, and resting on a delicate neck. Her hair was chestnut and combed in a fashion that hid some of her cheeks, with a bushy tail at the back held together with one of those Irish ribbons. Her eyes were the focus of attraction for anybody looking at her—green—they illuminated her visage, and at the same time, gave her sensual and fatal desirability.

'Please, my lady, welcome to my modest shelter, and be seated. I want you to know from the onset I do not approve of using women as an object of ransom. Therefore, you are here tonight, as my guest and I have no intention of treating you in any other way but with the respect due to you. I must add, I am shocked your grandfather would make you the item of trade. In Britain, we do not treat our female folk in such manner—women hold a special place in our society. The fact they give birth to children is regarded as one of the most sacred acts of life. They are also crucial in the formative development of our infants. Would you have some food with me?'

Bridgit spoke Gaelic, however she had learned Briton from several slave nannies who had raised her. She had become keen to learn so she could communicate playfully with her servants without her parents understanding it. It was a form of freedom.

'My Lord, I do not speak your language well. Please be indulgent to my grandfather. Piracy is a way of life on this island, and I *do* understand the pain it causes to your people. I will graciously accept your invitation to share some food with you.'

'Thank you. I am amazed by your proficiency in our language and I would like to take this opportunity to ask you to tell me more about your island.

'My Lord. Erin is a place where history, legends, and mythical occurrences blend into one another, and it is hard to discern the difference. We are realistic as well as surrealist, dreamers and superstitious, we feel we are unique... in short, the gods' favourites. Life is tough in this country, and we were always destined to struggle, but we think the gods impose the very struggle on us as a favour. We are independent people and do not like outside influences. My grandfather wants you and your troops off our land as soon as possible, and he has a responsibility towards his clansmen, even if it means I have to die for the freedom and the preservation of our ways of living; I am but a small price to pay. We are raiders, and nothing is going to change that. What we cannot find around here, we take elsewhere, and we see nothing wrong with that.

Cranadh looked at her all the while she spoke. He began to understand their mentality. He felt a deep attraction to the person with a voice and movements that were magnetising him... he fell under her spell. One of his chiefs came in the tent and wanted audience at once.

'My Lord, I have just arrived from Lahinch, and our fleet is on alert as we have seen some Irish ships, about fifteen of them, scouting in the distance.'

Cranadh held council and decided to retreat and check the town for any disturbances. Everything was quiet. The Britons thought something was awry and took action at once. They burned the village, packed their camp, and took Seamus, Bridgit and the twenty chieftains on their withdrawal to the coast. There by morning, they embarked their vessels.

The Britons' navy departed from the bay, drawing its attention to fifteen Irish ships to the north. Cranadh and Poher chose to engage and destroy as many as they could.

The Irish vessels were smaller and less numerous, the wind was coming from the southwest, and the strong current was heading north.

The fleet headed south, deliberately slow so as to entice the Irish into following them. Cranadh's flotilla was forming two lines, wide apart, fifteen boats in each. The Irish vessels caught up within half an hour; they were in a packed formation. Suddenly, the two lines of Briton ships turned in the opposite direction and quickly sailed north with the wind and the current in their favour. The Domenean fleet threw burning projectiles at the Irish, and quickly, ten of their vessels were on fire. Each Briton ship could hurl a dozen burning shots at once. There were scenes of carnage on the Irish crafts. Some of the burning fireballs landed in the sails and on the masts, resulting in the riggings falling on the sailors. Several Irishmen took burning slugs directly on the body and suffered horrible deaths. Some others, terribly injured by flames, tried to escape by jumping in the sea, where they drowned. The Irish could only toss spears, which invariably landed in the sea. Arrows were the only effective weapons. These darts mortally wounded several Britons, among them, a captain.

Cranadh's navy turned once more west-southwest, nearing the wind, always in two lines, and finished off the remainder of the Irish flotilla. Bridgit was on Cranadh's ship, locked up in his quarters. Poher gave the order to throw nineteen of the twenty chieftains and Seamus overboard, far enough from the coast they could not swim back. Some went to their death bravely, others had to be pushed and beaten or killed before being hurled in the water. Seamus himself died singing an old hymn. The remaining chief was put in a small boat offshore, a long distance away from Lahinch, so he could relate what had happened.

Less than a week later, the fleet was back in Kernow. It had been an expedition with mixed success. The pirates would understand they had to curb their incursions on British soil, but no slaves had been recovered, and they would be subjected to deadly retaliation. Bridgit was the only person brought back from Erin; Cranadh did not know what to do with her. He offered her the hospitality of the castle, to do as she pleased. He was attracted to her, but Cranadh also realised she was in pain, grieving the loss of her grandfather and countrymen. He, in a cowardly way, did not want to confront her.

Chapter Nine

Cranadh was getting weary. The punitive expedition to Erin had exhausted him, and he was not yet ready to face the reality of the political situation in Britain. He wanted to pause for a while to recoup his strength and intellectual faculties. Life was catching up with him, and the Kentish expedition had some sequels. A delegation of kings and chieftains from the east wanted to present Cranadh with their views of the situation which prevailed in south-east Britain. Hervey had a following in Kent, and the vacuums created by his slaying left the inhabitants bitter towards the rest of the Celts, and they were likely to side with the Saxons. The rest of the kingdoms were divided on the subject and wanted some assurances from the ruler of Domenea.

Cranadh thought trouble would come from the east so he met with their delegation. It made sense to listen to what they had to say. The visitors stated the Saxon threat was more significant than ever, and the notables felt anxious not to offend them further, but at the same time, they wanted promises Domenea would come to their help if requested. Cranadh interpreted the talks as an unwillingness to alienate the Saxons and not have him interfere in their affair unless they asked him to do so. He thought it an impossible request. In short, they would let the Saxons in, unless they felt they could not do otherwise. He believed it was an ambiguous and impracticable stance. Domenea, the Western kingdom, Cymru, and Cumbria were on their own. The Celts were splitting.

Cranadh realised the divergence. He would keep it to himself, let them talk, be civil but agree on nothing and let them leave. The situation implied his kingdom had to be ready for an incursion of a magnitude not seen since the Roman invasion. The very continuation of their way of life, civilisation, and institution was at stake.

Cranadh went back to his quarters; he needed to look at the sea for comfort, and reassure himself life was still good. He also longed for feminine presence, a need that had not manifested itself for a while. He wanted to find a pretext to see Bridgit and enquired of her whereabouts. She had gone for a walk on a shoreline path with one of the women designated to look after her. He put word out she was to meet him when she returned.

Two hours later, Bridgit showed up in the room Cranadh used to work and meditate on affairs of the state.

'Bridgit, how nice to see you. How have you been?'

'My Lord, a prized bird in a prized cage, is still a creature deprived of freedom. I am bored, lonely, and scared in the expectancy of news from you telling me what my fate is to be.'

'Well, here is a direct and honest answer. I summoned you because I need to confer with you, and I wish to know you better. I genuinely have not decided what I should do with you. As far as being a useful hostage and a leverage against Irish raiders, we both know that it is not a reality. I could send you back, and I may do that. On the other hand, I want you to teach me about the ways of your island. There is another reason... I must admit since my wife left me and even before our separation, I haven't had a feminine presence around me.'

'My Lord, I imagine you can request the company of any woman in your kingdom, and I expect they would fight to be with you. So, why me?'

'Your very question implies you are fishing for compliments. I like your aggressiveness, your self-respect. Although you are my prisoner, you keep your pride and are constantly pugnacious for your honour as Irish and a woman. Your appearance does not leave me indifferent. Any man would find you attractive. I have a request; would you accept to take a sea voyage with me and go to Armorica? It is the land of my mother, and I wish to visit part of it for several reasons.'

Bridgit felt her knees about to give up beneath her. The compliments and invitation were overwhelming. She collected herself, tried to look severe and in the gravest tone she could master said, 'My lord, out of respect for your mother, I will accompany you if my chaperon is also in attendance.'

The journey was to be a private affair. Domeneans often travelled to Armorica. The language was similar, and the two countries communicated without difficulty. Cranadh and his party of twenty would use one boat.

Three days later, on a sunny morning, they boarded the ship at the estuary of the big river, east of the palace. The boat was a merchant's vessel; sixty feet long, constructed like a bark, with the width a third of its length. The mast was situated at a third from the front, with a rectangular sail made of leather. The rudder was a big paddle fixed vertically starboard at the back the ship. It had no keel but extra heavy wood in the middle to stop it drifting. They wanted to go due south, but with the currents and the westerly wind, they aimed southwest.

It took them two full days to sight the coast of Armorica; they were more eastwards than intended. They sailed into a vast bay with a high rocky mount in the centre of the shoreline. The cliffs on the east side were granite topped with heather, ferns and green grass towards the western side; there were also granite cliffs with thick woods. They aimed for the high mount in the middle of the coastline. They navigated until they touched bottom about twenty boat lengths from the shoreline. The tide was going out.

The feeling of the inlet was magical; one could feel a huge spiritual presence. It was getting dark, and the group went ashore to set up camp for the night.

Cranadh told Bridgit about his mother, Annick. She was from the tribe of the Ossimi; never subdued by the Romans and the true inheritors of the Gaulish traditions. He also touched on the fact Armorica was particularly mystical for him and he tried to explain it to her.

'Armorica for me is the link to our Celtic past. Every time I come here, I have a bond with our old customs. The people here are closer to our traditions and history of our ancestral land to the east. The Armoricans are superstitious and humble. The landscapes, particularly the woods, give the impression they are full of spirits looking at us—sentient beings. The fauna instil the same feeling in me.'

Bridgit could see Cranadh was elated so kept silent, not wanting to interrupt the emotions he experienced.

The early hours saw Cranadh climb alone to the top of the high rock in the middle of the shoreline of the bay. It was not an easy ascent as the air was humid and the ground muddy. When he finally reached the summit, he was out of breath and his clothes were soiled from the mire but he felt close to the spirits of the land.

Cranadh drew his sword and raised it obliquely to the sky. Turning towards the south, where the bulk of the land lay, he shouted to the Heavens.

'Land of dark forests and sandy bays... please, accept us as your newfound brothers. We shall be one. Revival land of the Bretons, I call you Breizh!'

The circle was completed; nine hundred years ago, they left Gaul but were about to return. It was odd Cranadh was renaming a territory that did not belong to him. The radical thought had come as a result of many moments assessing the fact the Saxons would eventually take over, and in a not too distant future. He concluded if they wanted to keep their way of life, their freedom and traditions, they would have to emigrate, and what better a place than Armorica. He kept his reasoning to himself, judging it would seem too outrageous for his compatriots to understand.

Cranadh and his suite travelled the next day to pay a visit to his aging uncle, Erwan, in Landreger. Erwan, his mother's older brother, reigned over a small territory called Treger. They stayed four days.

Cranadh invited his uncle and some of his merchants, druids and artisans to make the voyage across the sea so the two countries could get closer to each other. After all, they were of the same blood, and it made perfect sense. Cranadh disclosed the situation in Britain to Erwan.

'You know uncle, as powerful as you might think Britain is, you must be aware the Saxon presence is dividing us. These barbarians should be ruthlessly sent back to their Teutonic land. Before, we were united as a nation, but now we are separated, and it makes us vulnerable. Before we realise, they will have conquered a third of the island and then it will be too late. I cannot fight my fellow Celts to bring them to reason, it would be too costly, and soul destroying.'

'I could send help. Just say the word.'

'Thank you a thousand times, but right now there is nothing to do; it might come to that in the not too distant future though if we get overrun. Instead of living in cohabitation with the Saxons, we will have to sail to other lands.'

'By Luth! If that happens, you know where to come. But, as far as I am concerned, all this is inconceivable. In Britain, you have rid yourselves of the Romans, here we had to be constantly aware of temporary attacks. We did adopt some of their ways in order to feign an appreciation of their ways.

'You are right, maybe I see too dark an outlook for the future.'

Chapter Ten

The trip to Armorica was just a memory. Cranadh and Bridgit had become closer. He was attracted to her features, and also her temperament. Her ways of politely arguing with him were extremely tantalising; she had a sarcastic way of disparaging him. Bridgit hated to admit it but she liked his attention. Here was a man, king of a kingdom, and her captor, no man before had ever treated her so well. After all, she was a granddaughter of an Irish clan chief from the west of Erin, which was insignificant in comparison with Connaught, Ulster, and Leinster.

At the winter solstice, after the trip to Armorica, Cranadh had invited Bridgit to attend the ancient ceremony of lengthening daylight. A huge feast followed the druidic customs; the meal served was by tradition, the most sumptuous of the year and throughout, musicians and bards performed Celtic tunes and stories. After the festivities, Cranadh invited Bridgit to his quarters using the pretext of discussing her future. She was nervous, not knowing from week to week what was held in store for her. The Irish maiden had grown fond of Cranadh; something in her body was sensitive to his physical presence. By the time they met, she was full of anticipation and anxiety.

Cranadh stood in the middle of the room and Bridgit in the threshold. She took two steps then paused. She read his facial expression and knew he was not going to discuss her prisoner status. His eyes gleamed, his mouth slightly open, and his cheeks flushed. He took half a step forward.

'I have been close, many times, in wanting to express the sentiments I have for you. I cannot bear my silence a moment longer. Bridgit, I wish we could see much more of each other. This situation of captor and prisoner does nothing to reflect the reality of my feelings. I want it to stop right now. You are free to do as you wish. You can move around the kingdom or return to Ireland. If you choose to stay, I will order you a proper household, with servants and men of arms to protect you.'

'My Lord, I appreciate your gesture. I shall be your subject, but I wish we were more forthright with each other and openly admitted our fondness for one another. I have no intention to go home. I want to explore your kingdom... with you if possible.'

Bridgit inched forward, as did Cranadh. He took her in his arms; their faces close. Their first loving kiss lasted long enough to release the suppressed passion. Containing the impulse no longer, Cranadh touched her left breast, she responded by grabbing his neck, pulling gently on his hair. Cranadh led Bridgit by the fingers to his bedroom, touching and caressing each other all the while. There, they became entangled in a mess of clothes, half undone. Before long, yhey lay naked, stroking and kissing each other's flesh. Making love occurred as reason for this eager longing they had held for one another. From that night on, they were lovers and inseparable companions.

The following spring, Cranadh and Bridgit became man and wife. Cranadh, his sense of history prevalent, took the opportunity of their union to arrange a gathering of all the Celts—Armoricans from Gaul, Welsh, nobilities from Britain, with the exception of Kent. The Irish presence was a feat he had accomplished. They sailed from Ulster, Connaught, and Leinster to see one of their own marrying the influential Briton. Jousting games were organised and indeed rigged so the Irish would be victorious. Cranadh's vision required a closeness to the Gaels—he needed them. Cooperation was advocated instead of pirating. The wedding of Cranadh and Bridgit was a matter of love but also a political statement.

Bridgit gave birth to their son, Konan, a few years later. At the same time, the Saxons were reported coming ashore in several new areas. As expected, Kent was the primary location for landing, and collaboration with the invaders was a fait accompli—Kent was lost. The south coast was threatened as well as the marshlands, north of the Tamesas.

The Saxons were not a homogeneous group. The tribes invading Kent were Jutes, from present-day Denmark, and Friesians from the islands of nowadays Holland. The Saxons in situ were from what is lower Saxony, between the rivers Weser and Elbe, what is now Schleswig-Holstein. They did not act in concert, and like the Celts, had no political hegemony.

On the British side, there were signs other local kingdoms might side with the Saxon invaders. At the same time, tribes from the Lundun areas north of the Tamesas and up the east coast to Alba were worried about the northern invasion from the Picts and Scots. They felt they were too weak to face an incursion and sought help from the Saxons. In their mind, hiring mercenaries was preferable to asking for help from the Western Celts. This would prove a colossal mistake.

The Irish were also intensifying their raids. The wedding of Cranadh to Bridgit, and his gesture of conciliation seemed to have been in vain.

The inevitable happened. Ewen, the king of the land north of Lundun, and the Oceanus Germanicus coast, started to negotiate with some Friesians about the danger caused by the Picts and Scots, who, in Ewen's belief, were about to invade his territory. The deal followed, if the Friesians were to fight the northern neighbours, they would be granted land north of the Tamesas estuary. It was more than these Teutons could wish for—as competent mercenaries, they contained the Scots by fighting them on their land. Cranadh, hopeless to intervene, was enraged. He could have fought Ewen and the Friesians. However, he was unsure what the reactions of the remaining eastern and southern kings would be, besides, his army was not big enough to take them on all at once so far from base.

The moment had arrived to form a concrete coalition of the kingdoms who wanted to survive as independent territories. Celts, through the ages, had produced notable traitors in their midst. Caesar had been helped by some Celtic tribes to invade Gaul. Ewen was of the same mould. The ego and self-interest of these traitors was bigger than Celtic hegemony.

To make matters worse for the Domeneans, the Irish were "stabbing them in the back", and Cranadh thought they should be brought into the fold to fight with the Britons, but that was a dream. Nevertheless, Cranadh, to secure his western border and coast, decided on a quick trip to Ulster to talk to their king.

A small party set sail. They created quite the surprise when they reached the castle of Kevin, the Ulster king. The court listened to Cranadh's plea for the realms of Erin to stop pillaging the west coast of Britain. Moreover, he asked them to provide some military assistance in case the Saxon threat became bigger than his troops could handle. In return, he promised to send them a respectable amount of tin and wine for a year.

Kevin told Cranadh he needed time to think about it. He could not believe his good fortune. The Ulsterman immediately called for his counsel to hold an impromptu session. He proposed the following.

'Clansmen! The gods of kind fate have delivered us Cranadh the Domenean. I do not have to remind you, a few years ago, he killed the men from Enistemon. Cranadh and his men will not return to their home. I suggest we let them go back to their ship after agreeing verbally to Cranadh's arrogant proposals. In the meantime, I will order six ships to sail, and as soon as the Britons are at sea, we shall attack them and sink their boats. Back in their country, they will think they perished in a storm. My good friends, there is no advantage in keeping them hostage, it would only create unwanted enquiries. We have no want to have to deal with the Welsh and the Kornish. As far as helping them, I cannot foresee any benefit. We have lived apart for centuries; the Scots are our cousins, not the Britons. Their troubles are not ours.'

An Irish monk, Gildea, awakened the Domeneans in the early hours of the night. He warned them Kevin had terrible deeds ready for them and they were in danger of perishing. He explained he was helping them as he was Bridgit's cousin. He travelled with them to the coast, and two days later they reached Cumbria in the North West of the Domenean Realm.

The Domenean diplomats all felt good to be on home ground. That part of the kingdom was separate from the rest of the realm. It was hilly, even mountainous, and green with numerous lakes. Caerwick was the main fort and town where Gwen had retired. Cranadh decided to stay at one of his vassal holdings near the coast. Three days later they were back at his castle in the south.

The expedition had determined the Irish were not concerned about the situation in Britain. Furthermore, it was of note to consider they would always try to avenge what they considered past humiliations.

Bridgit was surprised to see her cousin Gildea. She was saddened by the happening to her husband's endeavour to get a rapprochement between the two groups of Celts. Irish and Britons had lived far apart for many centuries. As far as the Irish were concerned, the Romans had stained the Britons. It was an erroneous belief, but it was their conviction.

Throughout the next five years, the Saxon expansion followed its course. War was inevitable, and Cranadh had to consider he might be killed in battle. His son was now nine, and succession to the throne would go to Gralon, Duke of Kernow, until Konan reached the age of seventeen years. In order to educate Konan, Cranadh had invited Gralon to live at Finnygook Castle, for the last two years. Cranadh agreed, with his council, the modalities of what would happen if he were to depart before his son was old enough to reign and Gralon was to assume regency in the transitional period.

The great confrontation between the Celts and Saxons, which had been looming for years, finally arrived. The forces faced off south of Sulis. The two encampments were situated on two hills distant by one-and-a-half miles in a north-south direction; the Celts occupied the northern rise. In between, stood a wood, a stream running through.

The Britons were mostly from the west, Cymru, and the northwest. Saxons, Kent, Lundun, and southern Celts represented the enemy. The Britons had more cavalry and archers while the Saxons had a mobile and disciplined infantry. There were about thirteen thousand troops on each side. The head of the Saxon forces was Manfrid. A warlord all his life, he was accomplished in many combat disciplines—maritime, skirmishes, frontal attacks, and large engagements—he was a redoubtable foe. Cranadh and his war council had heard of Manfrid's reputation. The Celts had spies in the invaders' ranks. Some Kentish and southern Celts, unable to betray the blood flowing through their veins, had been persuaded they would be of more use staying in the shameful allegiance and passing on intelligence.

Manfrid guessed the Britons would try to dislodge him from his high ground and lead him into the wood beneath. He had speculated they might try a flanking movement and judged it would take them at least six to seven hours to execute such a manoeuvre.

Both sides grasped staying put was not an option; the goal was to destroy the other. A fight *had* to happen.

Manfrid sent scouts on his flanks and rear to alert him of any enemy activity in those vicinity. Cranadh and his staff got wind of Manfrid's intention from a deserting Celtic scout. They started to send small but visible cavalry units into the Saxon's flanks and rear,-with the result it kept the Teutons concentrating on the perceived threats.

When night came, all the Britons moved quietly and suddenly to the edge of the wood facing their enemies' forces. They made sure there were signs showing they had departed towards the east and west instead of the south. The aim was to make the enemy believe they had started an enormous encircling tactical action. By dawn, Manfrid thought the Britons were on the move to try to surround him. He, therefore, sent a third of his troops to the east, south and west.

The surprise came around seven in the morning when the Britons launched a massive frontal attack on the depleted hill. They had a numerical advantage and swiftly decimated half the Saxon army. Troops Manfrid sent scouting did come back, but that did not change the outcome. Battles went on until the middle of the afternoon. Cranadh joined the mêlée after the initial frontal uphill assault. He was mortally wounded from receiving arrows to his chest and legs. He lost a lot of blood, and by evening he knew he did not have long to live. Gralon, Dugoat, Fanch and Pierik leaned over him as he lay on a red cloth. They gave him water to drink to ease his pain and difficulty speaking. They propped him up and rested his back on a blanket-covered saddle. In that relatively comfortable position, Cranadh spoke.

'The satisfaction of the day is our routing these savages and their Celtic traitors. The bad tidings... they will be back. The Teutons are even more stubborn than we are. I only have a few hours, if that, to live, so please listen to what I have to say. I have known for a few years now that our lineage is in danger. The terrible sadness is that we fight amongst ourselves. Remember my friends, far east of here, in the wooded hills of the continent, we were once all together; our traditions and beliefs originated then and there. If we have to conserve our heritage, we must get closer together as Celts so we can defend our traditions. If each tribe acts with selfish intent, we will lose it all. Unless that is understood, we are doomed. Other nations will use us; we will suffer the loss of our inimitable quality. Perhaps mine is an unrealistic dream but if Domenea is endangered, you must consider, in earnest, immigrating to Armorica. We are, with the Armoricans, the only Celts who understand we have to preserve the bond to the past. We hold all Celts in our affection, but they do not necessarily reciprocate the sentiment.'

Cranadh's lengthy speech gave him cause to cease momentarily whilst he took a sip of water before continuing his address.

'I am getting so cold, I am shivering, and I fear, my friends, I am losing consciousness. Poher, tell Bridgit and Konan my last thoughts were for them. Look after Konan. Pierik, my lifelong friend, my confidant, I would like to spend a few moments with you.'

The other three stepped back, making sure they would not hear what was said between the two companions.

An hour had not passed when Pierik got up and approached the others.

'All is consumed. Cranadh's last utterance before he departed for other Celtic worlds was in urging his successor to keep his subjects free and watch over his son as well as his wife.'

All his life, Cranadh had one main preoccupation: keeping the Celtic world, on the island, free of foreign interference. Britain was the last stronghold of the leading group of Celts who left central Europe nineteen hundred years ago. Britain was the last guardian of Celtic freedom. Cranadh died defending that autonomy. Gralon inherited a kingdom still under the menace of invaders. Domenea and Cymru were the only realms strong enough, and with determination matching that strength, to provide a powerful resistance against the Saxons. The other territories were too weak and would be acquiescent to the intruders.

After the defeat south of Sulis, the Saxons retreated to Kent and the Southeast. They deduced from their rout, more reinforcement had to come to Britain and overwhelm the Celts by sheer numbers. They realised the Celts were fierce warriors and the majority of the ones in the west would not surrender in their struggle for life.

After the passing of Cranadh, Gralon was immediately instated as Regent. His first task was to arrange his late leader's funeral. The ceremony took place in Sulis and was without pomp. All vassals were present. Cranadh's body was transported back to his palace of Finnygook. Along the road, many of his subjects, alerted by the news, were paying their last respects to the one who tried all his life to keep them free from foreign domination. Cranadh was buried, facing the line of the summer solstice, and in the old Celtic tradition, with his favourite chariot, sword, jewellery, and ceremonial clothes. The only concession to Christianity was a Celtic cross.

Bridgit was devastated. Cranadh had been a king, husband, confidant, and the father of her only child. He had always respected her Irish background. Cranadh was a student of the history and customs of her island and her people. He had told her there was a certain inscrutability about Irish people, something he claimed, he was not able to put his finger on. He put it down to the fact these Celts had been exposed to and had espoused the custom of the previous inhabitants of Erin. They had been separated for a long time from the rest of the race and as such, they were a suspicious and feral group.

Bridgit remembered the first moment she saw Cranadh. She had surmised, rightly, Cranadh was never going to abuse his rank. The transition from master to husband had been smooth. She felt very lonely and Cranadh was the closest human being to whom she could relate. Losing him would make her isolated. Domenea was, for Bridgit, more of a duty than an affection. She was the mother of the child who would be king. She had the responsibility, so she felt, to make sure he would be a good Briton. However, she was not likely to make him forget he was also Irish. Konan was too young to understand the significance of all this.

Gralon learned from Cranadh his mission was to prepare the ground for Konan. In the meantime, he had to carry on the work of protecting the kingdom and its subjects. The Domeneans, the Welsh and the entire west were on alert to defend themselves against an enemy who was determined to grab their land and subject them to slavery. Their last military victory was merely a respite in the struggle. Gralon had no intention to carry the fight to the Saxons. His idea was to build a line of forts along the eastern border of Domenea, from the Cotswolds to the sea, and also along the coast from Dorsetshire to Kernow.

Finnygook was still the principal seat of government, but Gralon preferred to reside in a fort at the estuary of a river, flowing north-south to the sea, named Cranadh in honour of the recently departed king.

Gralon did not have any children, so he looked after Konan with a lot of affection.

Bridgit was getting lonesome, and Gralon recommended she should visit Erin with Konan whenever she wanted. It was essential to expose the boy to his Irish culture as well as his British roots. She went back and forth to the island with her cousin, the monk Gildea, usually staying in monasteries.

Gralon and Cranadh had talked many times about the possibility of taking some Britons and settling them in Armorica. It had only been a wild idea but as Gralon knew Cranadh had family ties in Armorica, he felt it made sound political sense to introduce himself to the land of the Ossimi nobilities.

Gralon went across the sea with ten men and landed near Landreger. They met with Garach, the landlord and warlord of that part of Armorica. Garach was the son of the late Erwan, Cranadh's uncle. Garach's castle was on the bank of the river Leger. The Britons were invited to dinner, and both parties faced each other on opposite sides of a substantially large rectangular table; the witness of many a hearty feast.

'My Lord Garach, I want to thank you for receiving us. I know your father was a close relative of Cranadh, to whom he offered military assistance. So far, we have kept the Teutons at bay. But who knows when they will be back with ideas of destruction.'

'My dear Gralon, welcome. Britons will always be well received in my chiefdom. Our two nations are bonded by blood. Our language is similar, and our history has common ground going back to the great migrations, which brought us here many centuries ago. We have practised commerce with each other. Though one disparity remains... we are luckier than you, we live in the prettiest place on earth.'

'I appreciate you reminding us of our close ties. Cranadh, while alive, always emphasised the same truth. The situation in Britain is somewhat tense. We do not know how long we can stand the advance of the Germanic forces and their Celtic traitors, but we are about to build a system of defence. Furthermore, a new phenomenon is becoming apparent. People from the occupied territories and the traitor states are leaving and coming into Domenea—overcrowding on our lands could be a real problem in no time at all. There may come a time when sending some of our people to Armorica would not be implausible. At the present moment, I should like to exchange some views and feelings about the idea.'

'My chiefdom, Bro-Dreger could not accommodate any massive immigration. However, the inland of Armorica is much less populated. Could your people live on this type of terrain? It remains to be seen. The countryside is rugged, wooded, with deep streams and windblown uplands denuded of trees where nothing grows. Game is plentiful though. It is also a land of mysteries where many people believe strange occurrences take place at night. I would consider guaranteeing you a safe landing on the understanding you move on. I could even provide scouts to show you the way to the interior. As for the other chiefs, I can only guess their reactions. They will be sympathetic to your plight but will not be ready to share their living space. I hope you understand their circumstances. If you had to come and settle, you would have to conquer every inch. I will hold council with my people to decide if we can grant you safe passage. I would probably be considered a turncoat by the other tribes to let you in Armorica.'

'Our predicament is our own. Garach, I thank you for your forthright words. It helps, I am grateful to you. We shall wait until your committee ends its considerations.'

Gralon and his entourage went to their quarters. The regent was disillusioned by what he had heard. He was not expecting an affirmative answer from Garach. Nevertheless, by courtesy he waited.

As anticipated, Garach told him safe landing and passage would only be granted to the Britons at the rate of three ships a month. The Ossimi chief was letting himself off the hook. So, he thought.

The Britons sailed back, and on the voyage, Gralon developed a plan; they would have to send small squads, no more than five men each, to explore Armorica, find suitable places to live and how to get there. The immigration, if there was going to be any, would be effected without the approval of the Armoricans. The Britons needed to proceed as they saw fit and avoid bloodshed.

Gralon and his party reached the estuary and the River Cranadh; Penaravon was the name given to his headquarters. The castle was simple but functional and protected from the river and the land by fortifications made of stones and wood. Worrying news awaited them. Bridgit, Konan and Gildea were a week overdue from their latest trip to Erin. They were last known to be in the vicinity of Dunnleann. It was probably a kidnapping with the inevitable demand for ransom; that meant a search had to be organised and it had to be strong enough to inflict severe punishment on the perpetrators. All his life, Gralon had had to endure the piracy of the Irish. It was not going to be an expedition but a quick punitive invasion of Leinster. Leinster—because it had been proven, time and time again, the aggressors were from that region.

Fifty boats, loaded with foot and mounted soldiers, sailed from Braetoll. Fifteen hundred men were dispatched. Bridgit and Konan *had* to be found.

The expeditionary force went ashore south of Dunnleann. It reached the first village, rounded all the men present, and put them to the sword. They did likewise with four other villages. After the first two days, they had killed about six hundred men. On the third day they marched north toward Dunnleann and killed every male in two other villages. On the fourth day, a small detachment of armed cavalry and chariot men appeared from the north. The head of the group spoke at once, asking to see the leader of the invading army. Gralon conveyed in no uncertain terms that unless Bridgit and Konan were returned safe and sound, the killings would resume. The envoy responded it was the wrong way to go about it if they wanted to see them again. The Breton suspicions were well founded. Gralon did not hesitate in having the envoy and his escort assassinated, their bodies strapped to their horses, and the animals whipped so they would take their bloody burden from whence they came.

The reply was not long to arrive. A lone horseman was seen on a hill near the Breton encampment. He stretched his bow and launched an arrow with a small package tied to it. The wrap contained a small finger with a note in Irish:

If you want to see more parts of your little Breton bastard, you carry on with the massacres.

Gralon paused when he saw the bloody message. 'Fine, I guess I will have to meet with these rogues.'

Poher Dugoat was told to prepare a warring party with the principle goal of making contact with the head of these wretched people in order to negotiate. A neutral location, where an ambush was impossible, had to be found for the meeting.

Two days later, a place atop a hill was the rendezvous for a negotiation between the Irish and the Bretons.

The Irish clan leader, Culann was a rough-looking warrior. His life had been piracy on the high sea off the west coast of Britain. The Irish leaders considered him and his band great sailors, fulfilling a niche in the armed forces of the island.

Gralon was flanked by Poher and Fanch. Both enemy groups were a respective distance from the centre of the negotiating spot. Gralon spoke first.

'You kidnapped our queen, the young king, and her confessor. In response to your repeated acts of piracy in our kingdom, we retaliated and killed a few innocents, just as you have been doing for years in our lands. You feign shock... you cannot take the medicine you have inflicted upon us for decades, so you decide to blackmail us and send the finger of our young king.'

'I am not interested in listening to what we are or are not, what we did or did not. We have the three persons you want back. If you want them returned alive, you listen to our demands. You stop the massacres and give us three ships, moored at Dunnleann, within a week.'

'I am afraid you have done it this time. Do what you have to do with the three of them. Let us turn away for home and burn a few more hamlets and villages on the way back.'

'Do you want the bodies wrapped or just thrown to the sea?'

'The decision is yours.'

Both parties went their separate ways.

Gralon felt enough was enough, he could not accommodate the Irish any longer. After decades of pirating, taking Britons as slaves, and now keeping his queen and young king hostage, he thought there were limits to what one could tolerate. On the other hand, he could not let his young king languish in this land of rapacious heathens, even less, let him die. The Domenean force retreated to their camp, packed up and moved down to the coast where their ships were moored.

Gralon ordered Poher to take care of two assignments. The first was to round up one hundred and fifty villagers and keep them prisoner near their camp by the shore. The second was to see Culann, tell him he had won, and the three ships would be delivered outside Dunnleann. Fifty hostages per vessel would be on board. The heir to the throne, his mother and her confessor were to be rowed to the flagship of the Briton fleet, anchored half a mile out to sea. The main flotilla and the three ships supposed to be part of the ransom were loaded with captives. If any tricks were played by the Irish, they would burn the ships.

The day of exchange arrived—a small rowboat navigated toward the Briton command ship. The three precious hostages were soon on board and the small flotilla set sail at once. The three ransom prize crafts began to sink at once, the prisoners jumping off into the water. Gralon had ordered the three ships sabotaged. Big holes had been cut and plugged in the hulls, and a system of ropes had been installed so the outlets could be opened from a distance. The masts had been sawn so much the sail weight caused them to collapse. The Irish would remember Gralon for quite a while.

Chapter Eleven

When Gralon reached Kernow he realised the Irish trip was leaving a nightmarish imprint in his mind. He was left wondering if it had actually happened.

The expedition had been necessary but was a distraction. The Saxons were still pushing in from the east. Cranadh had been right, more Celtic chieftains were siding with the intruders. Nothing had been done concerning an emigration to Armorica. A few sailors had circled the peninsula, nothing more. Gralon, as Regent, saw it his duty to explore ways of eventually relocating the people of Domenea to Armorica. Although not his initiative, he was convinced it was a plausible solution. He dreaded contemplating what it might involve.

The task had to be well planned. The move had to be decisive without wandering around, the invaders had to know exactly where to go, and settle. Gralon had no illusions, wherever they would decide to establish themselves, the natives would not accept them. Armed conflicts would be inevitable.

The exploration started west of Landreger; it was the location of Cranadh's invocation to the gods for finding a new homeland for his tribes. Some investigation had already taken place, and it was auspicious for settling. There were long beaches, rivers, forests, and river estuaries. The only factor missing was fertile fields for agriculture.

At a day's march to the west where Cranadh landed, there was the estuary of a large river; upstream were natural harbours, providing relatively easier access to the backcountry.

Gralon put a soldier navigator, Stivell, in charge of surveying Armorica. The primordial knowledge needed was population sizes, their organisation, their military strength, what they lived on, their attitude towards possible Briton settlements, their language, education, and culture. Although the Celts living in Armorica had never succumbed to the Roman ways, there were, nevertheless, various degrees of assimilation. Their judicial system, however, was similar to that of the ancient Gauls, and therefore identical to the Britons'. By far, the most critical information had to be the comprehension of the feelings of these tribes, they were ethnic brothers but nevertheless strangers.

Stivell and Gralon left the Cranadh estuary to go on a fact-finding mission. A few days later, they made contact with a chieftain, Leann, in charge of a tribe inhabiting the estuary of the river, west of the big rock—the Moraber region.

Gralon, unlike Cranadh, was not a visionary nor did he have a compelling moral urge to keep Celtic homogeneity alive. He was a workhorse—it had been bestowed upon him to accomplish a mission, and he would use all the tools available to him. Cranadh would have chosen the path of honour and dignity. Gralon, on the other hand, would be more efficient and would exploit every avenue presented to him. The Irish episode had shown an insight of his capability.

Gralon perceived Leann a man who needed to be a "big fish in his little pond" and he would play on it to the utmost. There was no doubt in Gralon's mind that without cooperation from the local tribes, there would not be any durable peaceful cohabitation. The Britons would have to expropriate the Celtic Armoricans, and they would dispute it. A system of compensation would have to be established. Gralon could be creative on the subject, and so he opened a dialogue with the tribal chief.

'How many of your people do you suggest bringing to the area?'

'Ten thousand.'

'Ten thousand? It is more than the actual inhabitants of our region. What you propose is an invasion.'

'Precisely, we would take over your life as you have known it.'

'So why should I let you land in the first place?'

'Because if you don't, we will demolish and scorch your tiny paradise in no time at all. Mind you, it will be messy, and I would rather cooperate with you and provide incentives to make us welcome.'

'Expand on the subject.'

'I can give you tin, ships and let you marry one of our noble girls.'

'What guarantees would be in place?'

'None, except, the fact you are talking to us makes your destiny and ours undeniably tied to each other. After all, we are not that bad, we are a much bigger tribe, a nation almost. We can bring you a lot of proficiency. Imagine, you could be the first of many to gain from our culture, our quality of life.'

'What about my freedom?'

'You can be your own master in a stinking pig pen or follow the trend in a rose garden. That is your choice.'

'So in practicality, what does it mean for us? What do you want? Come to the point.'

'We want you to give us some land where we can live our own lives, and not bother you. Our people and your people can mix. You will benefit from our commerce with the rest of the continent.'

'I do not accept such a notion. Your assets are good as long as you stay in Kernow. Once here, you will have nothing. I will tell you what you want... you want to come here, use my land as a base, do away with us and conquer the rest of Armorica. It will not happen unless I am an equal partner and we share the conquest of the country.'

'You want to use us to claim the rest of Armorica. That will not come to pass. We just want some land from you, and we will pay handsomely. This will be our stepping-stone, and once we have more territory, we will go away. We need to leave Kernow because we are running out of options to keep the Saxons at bay. Our coming to Armorica is humanitarian.'

'Nevertheless, it looks like an attempt to organise a conquest to me. Your nation is not wanted here. However significant your compensations, you are not welcome in this land. I have no desire to be remembered as the one who let the Britons in.'

'I underestimated you, and I respect your views. Our goals are the same, you are looking after your tribe and I, after mine. The sheer size of my peoples can make me take action, which could annihilate your very existence. I need a landing space and here, just where you dwell, is the preferred location. Farewell Leann.'

The Britons crossed the sea back to the Cranadh estuary. Despite Leann's protests, Gralon had his landing place determined. He still needed to know more about the interior of Armorica. Information teams were tasked with gathering intelligence discreetly over the coming year. The ideal situation was to land in Moraber, defeat Leann and move towards a suitable place to settle. They needed to know where to deliver battle to guarantee their safety. Their power was in number. Armorica was full of small tribes lacking central organisation. It was necessary to land as many soldiers as possible to be the most significant armed force in the peninsula, pierce their way through and outflank or bypass most of the inhabitants.

A major topic on Gralon's government agenda was the future emigration to Armorica. One might have thought it premature to leave Britain. The Domeneans did not want to have to do it under duress nor in haste. Armorica would be an expedition first, a conquest, second. Yet again, a fleet of military transports and protection escorts had to be built. Two hundred units were to be constructed. The estuary of the Cranadh with all the woods surrounding it, would be the site. A plan was starting to take shape. A complete restructuration of the armed forces took place to adapt for a large-scale amphibious operation.

The boats were of standard contemporary construction and able to sail in shallow waters. They were of three categories. One hundred vessels carried forty foot soldiers, ten horses, and cavaliers with their equipment. Sixty ships transported thirty-five mounted soldiers, their horses, and five chariots. Forty boats had thirty men with supply and command personnel. All in all, the entire force comprised four thousand foot soldiers with one thousand cavaliers scouting and supporting them, a mobile force of two thousand, one hundred mounted soldiers with three hundred chariots, and twelve hundred men guaranteeing supplies and communication between the groups.

Chapter Twelve

It had been a year and a half since the meeting with Leann. The fleet and invading force were ready. Gralon and the armada sailed on a gloomy morning, a day after Samhain, the start of the Celtic New Year. The planned build was accomplished. Starting an invasion at this time of the year was thought the most suitable period, given there would be fewer people working the countryside so the element of surprise would be substantial.

The plan was implemented, all the expeditionary force landed in less than two days and moved west towards Moraber. Leann's navy had about fifty units, worrisome to the invading Domeneans. One day later in a synchronised move, the Briton foot soldiers and cavaliers burned Leann's ships and ransacked the storage buildings, but left the population relatively unharmed. They moved back towards the Big Rock (Ar Bras Roch) where they had landed. They built a small fort at their port of entry and started walking south toward the interior. They followed the course of a stream with a narrow road alongside and reached higher ground. A bigger camp was built and secured close to where they found some Roman vestiges and coins in a quarry; they called their camp Treduder (Dark Soil Field).

Gralon was morose; the enterprise of occupying Armorica conflicted him. He worried he was spreading himself sparsely. Back home in Kernow, the refugees from Saxon-occupied territories were increasing in numbers. That fact reassured him he was doing the right thing in seeking new lands. The trouble was he needed settlers and right now he only had soldiers who were looking for a fight, and he had to contain them. The people of Armorica were their blood brothers. Much of the land was inhabited and what was left for the taking was naturally not in the best regions.

Gralon was unsure what was inland. The Domenean scouting parties had stuck to the coast and to the south lay a gulf where the Venete lived. He set out to achieve two tasks—the soldiers were to assess the land for agricultural use, as well as, secure the land around Treduder in a circle of several miles, and they were to go south and explore the interior. Poher was given the assignment with four hundred mounted men and two hundred foot soldiers.

The interior was supposed to be wild, inhabited by mystical creatures. The Celtic mythology had transported itself from the ancestral land, left a long time ago, to those high windy plateaus, dark forests and tenebrous lakes.

The expeditionary force was to be tested only a couple days after they left Treduder. Some of their horses were missing; yet nobody heard anything. They felt observed yet saw no-one. The soldiers sensed something mysterious and disturbing about the country... it was just peasants seeing the opportunity to increase their stock. In every Celtic society, casts were present, and those who stole the horses were the lower end of the scale. They were more in fear of their masters than armed intruders. The invaders had not considered such a thought. To be the hostile invader was something new for the Domenean. They needed space to live, but they had to take it from other Celts.

The march to the South continued. They crossed wild country, negotiating thick forests, cleared lands, rocky outcrops, and untamed streams. Horses were stolen nearly every night, yet they could neither see nor hear the perpetrators. The men were getting frightened; they started to believe a mystical power was working against them. The feeling became real when soldiers began disappearing. After a week of travel, half of their mounts had vanished along with one hundred men. Nevertheless, Poher decided to press onwards south. Wooded uplands and rocky denuded hills followed deep wooded streamed valleys. The attitude of the small army changed. Whenever they saw a hamlet or any of the inhabitants, they destroyed both. They always felt stalked.

This was a bad start for an endeavour supposed to find a new homeland. The attractive landscape gave pleasant sensations to most soldiers; the land was numinous in such a way it linked reality to the imaginary. Poher considered aborting the mission. Losing one-sixth of his men was bad omen enough, but the rest were becoming superstitious and tentative. For soldiers, to fight is natural, but once morale is lost, they become numb.

There was a Roman road in a north-south direction; it was a faster march on an open thoroughfare and reduced the possibilities of ambush. The element of surprise had vanished.

They reached the south coast of Armorica within a week and took a few days to rest and regroup. A local chieftain came to inquire after them. Poher was understood in his native language, and when he was not, he spoke in Latin. The chieftain wanted to know if they were passing by on their way to the south of Gaul and if they were going to fight for the Romans having trouble with some Germanic tribes. (Celts and Insular Celts were known to rent their services as mercenaries for the Romans.) Poher lied and told him it was so. They resumed their journey and followed the coast eastward.

Before they came to Waen, they noticed a huge lake; actually a gulf opening to the sea as it had tidal movement. Under no circumstances did they want to encounter the Venete; these long-time warriors, sailors and merchants were a nation in their own right. Hence, the Domenean went inland and decided to head north where they could see tree-covered highlands.

Poher decided to lead his men back to Treduder using a different itinerary, that way they could discover new territories.

The small-revivified army was moved into the interior; the countryside was gentle. They reached a grassy plateau, suitable for agriculture and with a small river nearby. Poher named the sparsely populated area Treveleg (Field of Priest) because he could see a church steeple above a line of trees. It was the first space they encountered suitable for a Domenean settlement and to sustain life. The concept of how Armorica was to be settled was not evident in Poher's mind however, he was sure Gralon had a strategy.

The Briton force continued their march northwards for two weeks. They went through wild forests, high plateaus, and thickly wooded river valleys. Their progress was slow due to the terrain. They did not get attacked; they had heightened their awareness and very few people lived in these parts. They finally reached the north coast on a vast bay where tides retreated along great distance; the Bay of St Brieuc. A river had its estuary on the west side of the gulf. They turned west, avoiding Bro-Dreger, the fief of Cranadh's mother. Three days later, they were back in Treduder.

The expedition had been a happenstance with reality. Moving to Armorica was not going to be a walkover. Even without significantly organised armies, the Armoricans would make the entire invasion a thorny scheme; made harder as the present inhabitants were similar peoples to them and would fight to keep what they had. The Britons, on the other hand, wanted to live side by side in peace. With this new information, Gralon gathered an incursion without conflict was not realistic so he reassessed his plans. Instead of a massive concentration of troops, he thought to divide his army into small groups of no more than a hundred men. These groups would be self-sufficient and explore the interior; their goals to gather intelligence and relay back to headquarters. The other mission was to dismantle the local structure by eradicating local chiefs and people of influence. The plan was to make Armorica as vulnerable as possible so when the main thrust came, it would be done quickly, with minimal resistance.

Chapter Thirteen

Enervi was from the northernmost part of Domenea. He was one of the squad commanders due to explore part of Armorica. He had been with Poher of Dugoat on the last exploration of the future colony. He requested to join a group going back to the plateau named Treveleg. He had sixty men under his command; forty foot soldiers and twenty mounted. Half the mounted squad was supply chariots and scouts.

It took a week to reach Treveleg where they wished to establish a fortified camp, and proceeded to meet the sparse inhabitants of different hamlets. The locals did not know what to make of these foreigners especially as they were heavily armed.

Treveleg's headman was named Gallix. Enervi explained his squad was going to explore the countryside. He held back to say he was on a discovery mission with the goal of bringing people from Kernow to live in their neighbourhood. He also omitted to mention the probable confiscation of some of their lands. He left out the fact the new arrivals would have to be fed and given shelter thus changing the economic makeup of the region. Inevitably, conflicts would transpire, and the probability they would have to be resolved by force was likely.

The locals' religion was different—their priests were more obedient to the pope in Rome than the ecclesiastic organisation in Domenea. Welsh and Irish monks, who were part of the invading tribes, had a loose connection with Rome. Papal obedience did not exclude the old druidic religion and it was more prevalent in Armorica where it mixed with Christianity.

Enervi established his camp on top of a plateau. It was semi-fortified; secured enough to prevent surprises but open enough to encourage exchanges with the local population.

Gallix advised Enervi the ancestors of the people living around Treveleg were a combination of Venete and Celt; the latter had arrived about a thousand years ago. He pointed out there were iron mines nearby. Smelting of the ore had been possible with all the thick forests around. He further explicated some of the woods had been cut down to provide agricultural land. Breeding cows for meat and milk, and pigs and fowl were also part of the agrarian way. Streams full of trout were present in the narrow-wooded valleys. The landscape was not flat by any means. The Romans had tried to plunder the region, but tacit non-cooperation had discouraged them from staying, and they had remained in Waen. Enervi could not help thinking Gallix had given him all the more reason to justify the Domeneans settling around Treveleg.

A vast, dense and mysterious forest lay north east of Treveleg. Called Broellian, it meant "Country of the Mist". According to the natives, both good and evil spirits, and mythical human beings were purported to dwell inside. Several times, the soldiers noticed the villagers taking the direction of the woodland. Enervi asked Gallix to lead him into the area but was refused as the location was a sanctuary for ancestral descendants alone. Bringing strangers would upset the spirits, souls, and hermit priests and priestesses living there. Enervi did not insist. The same day he held council with his lieutenants to explain the necessity to explore happenings in Broellian, the so-called sacred wood.

The plan was to hide on the outskirts of the forest, wait, then follow the men and women going into the inner sanctum. A small squad of four, including Enervi, was to complete the mission. Enervi stressed if they did not know what was going on in Broellian, they would never understand the natives and less able to govern them. He wanted to identify if a druid or spiritual leader was giving commands, telling the indigenous inhabitants how to conduct themselves towards the newcomers.

Favourable circumstance arrived, and under cover of thick vegetation, the squad followed a small group into a distant clearing full of huts and small stone edifices. In the centre of all was a field of thick grass. At first, they were unable to establish what the forms lying in the grass were doing. With closer examination, they perceived mass ritual copulation. The squad's initial astonishment turned to derision, then disgust and sheer curiosity.

Enervi and his men ventured back to Treveleg without being noticed by the actors of the debauch. Enervi saw Gallix and related his recent observation. The head-man was unmoved, knowing the rituals would have been discovered sooner or later.

'This is our private affair and tradition. The most potent of the men folk, and most fertile of our women folk are involved in these ceremonies to create a robust native tribe. We leave nothing to chance. The family of the female and her legal husband, not necessarily the biological father, raise the newborn from these brief carnal unions.'

'Does this create jealousy amongst families?'

'It does... some become attached to their ceremonial partners. Ablon, the druid, determines the partnerships. The Christian priest, Bodlan, has no part in all this.'

Enervi approached Bodlan; he was native to the village but had been to Rome and was suitably distressed about the old ways persisting in the village.

'I am myself a sinner. All traditions concerning the mating of compatible couples for bettering the line are causing much stress among the villagers. It takes up at least half of the consultations I have with my people. It is not healthy. I could work with you to try and eliminate the practice. We have never favoured mixing with neighbouring villages. Were that to be encouraged, it would solve their fixation with getting the healthiest children and would stop this abusive and sensual practice.'

'Why do you say sensual?'

'It is nothing else than a pretext for orgies. Much alcohol is usually consumed during these sessions. I know when I marry people, under the vows of Christianity, the unions are supposed to be a lifelong affair. The people have a hard life, and their only distraction is having sex with people other than their spouse. It is titillating for them, at least for a while, but then it becomes a source of conflict, jealousy, and envy. Life ultimately becomes more complicated.'

'I see, the people have a predilection for the old ways. Myself, I like the old ways, but those institutionalised orgies are just too much.'

All the prodding by the visitors was irritating Gallix. It started a spontaneous demonstration of hate towards the strangers, and he voiced it to Enervi.

'You, the invaders, have intruded our circle of life. You, soldiers from across the seas, do not belong here, you are outsiders. You cannot judge us. It would take you years to understand us. Frankly, I cannot guarantee your safety if you stay here.

Following the outburst, Enervi told his second in command, Fanac, to withdraw to their semi-fortified camp outside the village.

Having made a safe retreat to their makeshift fort, Enervi conferred with Fanac.

'We are not here to blend with their ways, we are here to establish a settlement for our people. We could try to assimilate and be accommodating, but it would be a waste of time. They will consider us invaders whatever we do. Gallix is the keeper of those perverted habits. My next move is to get rid of the chief, the druid, and the priest. When the druid Ablon comes back in the village, take a few soldiers and kill him. Dispose of the body so he cannot be found. Anyway, enough words.'

'There is no need for several men. I will do the job myself.'

Fanac went to take care of his mission and finally located Ablon. The druid was in meditation and invocation under a tree on a hill nearby.

'Hi, holy man. Enervi, my superior, has sent me to slay you but have no fear, I am not going to do you any harm. I just want you to listen to what I have to say. On our island, the conditions are overcrowded. We are here on a mission to establish settlements for our people. Although most of us have nothing against you, some will not let you get in their way. In other words, you are unimportant. I beg you, take a few people and disappear for a while. I will send for you as soon as it is safe to return.'

Fanac went back to Enervi; the two men started arguing about Ablon who was nowhere to be seen.

'You, Fanac, are an incompetent soldier. How could you let that druid escape from our grasp? Or perhaps you are too weak to execute such a deed. Go and bring Gallix to me.'

Fanac did so but was quietly horrified at the fate of the chief.

When Gallix arrived in front of Enervi, he was immediately nullified. Enervi reached for his knife, and was about to plunge it into the heart of the Armorican, but Gallix managed to free himself and reached for Enervi's wrist; a struggle ensued. Gallix threw Enervi on the ground. Fanac, seeing the scene, tried to pull Gallix off Enervi and found he had no alternative but to stab Gallix; in a split second, Enervi freed himself by throwing Gallix aside. Fanac was caught off guard by the body of Gallix moving towards him, lost his balance, and while falling, he inadvertently caught his knife across Enervi's throat; the slash was deep and caused instant death. Fanac at once realised the tragedy. As Gallix tried to escape, he was struck dead by other soldiers.

Fanac knew he would be unable to explain what happened; he took his horse and disappeared before anyone could react. His relationship with Enervi had always been confrontational, and everybody knew it, trying to explain the mortal wound would be indefensible at best. Too many would interpret the events as a seized opportunity by Fanac to avenge his repeated humiliations from his superior.

The Treveleg expedition was suddenly in jeopardy. On the occupiers' side, their leader was dead and the second in command had vanished. The rest of the Domenean decided to leave and go back north towards their main base. When they reached Treduder, Poher was visiting the camp from across the sea, and wanted to know what had happened. He heard a pitiable story. The Armorican were not to be subdued as quickly as originally thought.

Chapter Fourteen

Gralon looked to the estuary of the river, his expression pensive. His mind was reacting to the various reports he had received in the last week. Penaravon, the capital of Kernow, was a gloomy place these days. The kingdom was under attack from the east and also the west. The Saxons were getting organised to deliver revenge. Gralon was in a dilemma—either show real resistance towards the Saxon marauders, or simply contain them to secure crossing to Armorica.

The idea of purposely abandoning some land to assure a safe retreat and passage was in itself hard to endure for a proud Celt. The Welsh kingdoms had notified Gralon they would never abandon their lands. For them it was different, they lived among the mountains with a natural barrier, so it was easier for them to make a stand there. Also, they were much less numerous than the Domenean. The northern part of Domenea was the least affected by the invaders' push.

The Irish, those treacherous Celtic cousins, were banking on the fragility of the situation for the Britons. Intelligence from Armorica was mixed. The settlements on the northern coast of Armorica were relatively stable; anything inland was precarious with many reports of attacks on the troops. A landing had to take place on the southern coast to act as a pincer movement, but it would be a massive undertaking.

Gralon decided enough time had been lost in trying not to be at odds with the natives. He envisaged colonising the north coast would be logistically easier; from these settlements, he would pierce through the interior. The clergy could be used to establish a nucleus of parishes with the help of the soldiers and the collaboration of sympathetic local nobilities. The native population would be kept aside in the early stages.

Something else preoccupied Gralon's mind. Konan was now seventeen. He was well educated; he had tutors who taught him fine art and philosophy. On the subject of religion, Pierik had taught him the old Celtic ways. Various monks inculcated Christianity—some Irish, some Breton—but Efflam, his father's confidant, was the most influential.

The most significant impact on the young king was from his mother Bridgit. Despite all her years in Kernow, she was still a daughter of Erin. She impressed upon her son although he was a Briton, he had Irish blood in him. The boy was just as versed in Irish sagas and history as those of his own kingdom. Bridgit told him he could have a role in both countries when he came of age. She was not keen on immigrating to Armorica; she felt Kernow was the ancestral land and if there were to be a coronation of her son, it would be in Finnygook, the home of Cranadh's castle.

Gralon was not set on staying Regent. He sincerely wanted Konan to become king, but thought for the prince to take the reins in the present circumstances would overwhelm him. He therefore decided to have Konan crowned, but would stay as chancellor until he was satisfied the young king could take over, which could take several years. Gralon informed Bridgit about his resolution; her reaction was a happy one.

Gralon and Bridgit both started to work on the protocol. The guest list, as always in those affairs, was a delicate task. The Welsh would be invited, as would the Celtic kingdoms east of Domenea that were not subjugated to Saxon rule. Breton's chieftains were to be approached. Pictish tribes were to be contacted and an olive branch extended to some Irish. An envoy was even sent to Rome.

The king-to-be was nine years old when his father died. His mother, Efflam, and Gralon had always talked positively about Cranadh, however they were mindful not to sanctify the dead monarch.

Konan was of average height, on the slim side. All the exercises and combat practices had not sculptured his body into a muscular soldier, nevertheless, he had a lot of nervous energy, was a swift runner, and a superb horseman.

Penaravon, on the western bank of the river Cranadh, was the place where the druidic rite would be performed, followed by Finnygook Castle, the site for the Christian crowning coronation. The envoy from Rome was the one to place the crown on Konan's head. The Curse of the Rhoem was not forgotten, and the old gods had to be included in the coronation.

Konan was level-headed about it all; his mother was his political tutor. She had reminded him at all times, he would be the only Celtic sovereign who could bridge the gaps between all the tribes and kingdoms. Irish, Britons and Armorican blood ran through his veins.

These two ceremonies would be the last of their kind, although the participants had no way of knowing it at the time. The Roman Empire was crumbling, the Germans and Vikings were emerging as the new masters, and the Celts were surviving the best they could.

The druidic coronation took place by the river Cranadh; every Celtic nation was present. Two thousand people were in attendance, men and women standing side by side and all clothed in long white robes—wearing the same attire symbolised equality. In the centre of the huge field, a Triskell, a threefold sign with circumvolutions representing earth, water and air, had been scraped on the ground and filled with crushed white seashells. From the Triskell radiated a path to the east and one to the west. The spectators were four rows deep in a vast circle.

Konan appeared from the east, walked down the path, and skirted the Triskell in a clockwise manner to the south. He then proceeded to follow the path to the west, retraced his steps towards the centre and went to the northern most point. He laid down upon the soil, facing the grass, his head to the south. Only the sound of birds and the wind could be heard. Pierik, the head druid, appeared. His head was shaved half-way down his skull, his long beard was flowing in the wind and he held a crown of ivy in his left hand. He walked from the east across the Triskell, went west to the end of the path then retraced his paces to the centre of the Triskell. He stood, facing north and towering over Konan who was still prostrate on the ground. Pierik stood there for a while in uninterrupted silence. The druid turned to the east and lifted his arms to the sky.

'Teuta, god of all Celts, we are here today to present you with our young king, Konan of Domenea. The Rhoem has, for a long time, cursed our tribe. By leaving our ancestral land, we offended you. We went west, but we are symbolically retracing our steps to the centre of your realm. We are your subjects; we do not forget you are judging us. By standing in the middle of the Triskell, we beg your forgiveness, seek your guidance and venerate your spirit. We pledge to stay united, help one another, be proud of our roots and traditions. Teuta... I offer you Konan.'

Konan rose up; his face was red and puffy, and he looked dazed. He genuflected; with his right knee on the ground, Pierik placed the crown of ivy on the young king's head. The spectating crowd erupted in cheer.

The druid walked the path to the east, Konan behind, followed by Bridgit, Gralon, and Poher. Horns resounded in the background—tunes that chilled the spine of the assembly, echoes of the past, reminding it the connection to ancient times not to be taken lightly. All broke rank and dispersed quietly... all looked grave.

The Christian ceremony was to take place at Finnygook Castle late afternoon. The pope's envoy was undoubtedly the most important and revered person. The coronation organising committee thought it a positive diplomatic move to have him crown the King. The Celtic Church had momentarily forgotten its significant differences with Rome.

Stands draped in black and white fabric had been built. The ceremony was taking place on a lawn outside the northern wall of the castle. The Roman cardinal was already sitting in a golden throne. In the seats to his right side were all the Domenean—nobilities, soldiers, members of every trade, and in a symbolic gesture, commoners from every corner of the realm had been picked to show their King cared about them. To the churchman's left sat kings, dukes, and warlords from Erin, Armorica, Cymru, Britain, Alba, and members of the clergy.

Konan was waiting on the west side of the wall. The Celtic crowning ritual had affected him. The gravity of the title bestowed upon him was reinforced and the Christian ceremony was confirmation responsibilities were coming his way, rapidly and solemnly. He understood what they meant for him and his people. The faint recollection of his father made him ever more solemn. Conversely, thoughts of his mother, Gralon, and Efflam made him smile and his mind wandered.

Celtic hegemony has cost me one little finger already. The bloodline of our ancestors has travelled a long way. All my family, councillors and subjects expect me to lead them across to Armorica. I am not sure it is the right thing to do. Gralon has told me many times our cousins across the sea are making us less than welcome. Who can blame them? They can see we are going to take their land, and they are going to make us suffer for it.

All my life I have heard about this great movement of emigration. Why have we given up thoughts of fighting these Germans, after all, my father beat them last time they met? I realise circumstances have changed; nowadays they are more or less at home in the east of Britain. The Welsh and Picts have no intention of moving away from their land; the Saxons are not a direct threat to them. To spare our people emigration might be the sensible thing to do. A long fight for survival or resistance could kill us as a nation. So we are saying, 'Saxons, you can have it'; we want to stay strong, and we are leaving for a place where we can be ourselves. Maybe it is the pattern of our civilisation, instead of fighting a costly battle, we move and survive?

Horns and trumpets announced the start of the ceremony. Konan slowly walked towards the Roman prelate; walking east, he could see the last rays of the sun projecting his shadow on the grassy floor. He thought it funny to get crowned at sundown. *Was it the extinction of an era or the end of one period and the start of a new?* These thoughts disturbed him, and by the time he reached the cardinal and prostrate himself flat on the ground, he wondered how he got there. The Celtic ceremony felt real to him, the religious one did not. The pomp had affected him, and he perceived the peers were judging and evaluating him as a future ally or foe.

The cardinal was the master of ceremony and invited Konan to kneel. He declared in Latin that God, his son Jesus Christ, and the Holy Spirit granted Konan the honour to guide his people. He was to use that gift the best he could in Christian manner to be the intermediary between the Holy Trinity and his subjects. The new leader was to reign under the title of Konan the First. The Holy Communion took place. Gralon passed the crown of Domenea to the Roman envoy who in turn laid it on the young man's head. The headgear was made of bronze, three equidistant Celtic crosses with serpentinite stones from Kernow encrusted around them.

Konan reaffirmed he was a loyal subject of God and his duty was to lead his kingdom in a Christian manner. Latin was the language used, and it made the oath surreal as though the words were not his. The Irish most likely would not understand nor the Picts, only a few of the Welsh, Armorican, and Domenean would take in some of the meaning. The new King could not help thinking it a broad farce. The Celtic ceremony felt so right yet now an intruder from Rome, dictating a code of ethics nobody respected, had performed the Christian liturgy. *Was it custom, was it fear of displeasing continental powers? Who knew?* Gralon and Efflam believed in the political wisdom of it all. Konan deemed he would not have to abide by the oath but at the same time, he felt it bad luck to ignore and renege it.

The moment had come for Konan the First to perform the first task of his royal duty. He ceremoniously walked the alley formed by the all the dignitaries—he waved his left hand and his right hand alternately, nodded his head and bowed his torso to the left and the right.

The feast took place at Finnygook Castle. Konan had insisted upon it in memory of his father. The courtyard interior had been transformed into a huge dining hall with space for the ensuing spectacles due to follow. Konan sat at the main table raised up from the floor and swathed behind in huge drapes depicting armouries of the Domeanean provinces. A large silver-coloured Triskell hung at the highest central point. Music was always crucial in any Celtic gathering. Fiddles, flutes, and shepherd bagpipes played continually. An enormous amount of meat was roasted and grilled, cabbages and stews were available, wine poured from numerous amphorae and alcoholic malt drinks were bubbling and served lukewarm. Konan sat with his mother on his right and Gralon on his left. Efflam, Gildea, Pierik-and Poher were also present. The head Pict, Irish, Armorican and Welsh sat at the headboard.

The frenetic music, wine, arguments and loud talks made for the cacophony of a fair on market day. The inevitable fights started. A strong contingent of soldiers was present to ensure the different nations would not begin hostilities. It was a regular occurrence amongst Celts for any quarrel initiated under the influence of alcohol to become a matter of life and death quickly for the party who took offence. The cause of such offence could be something so minor as the performance of a horse; any issue deemed to damage the 'victim's' honour. For centuries, countless Celts died over reasons which seemed pathetic once sobriety returned. Nevertheless, deaths of a partner or family members were never forgotten, even less forgiven, and lasted for decennia. The crowning of Konan, although a solemn occasion, was no exception. By four o'clock in the morning, ten cadavers had been removed from the floor—eight Domenean, one Armorican and one Pict.

Konan had left the mayhem by two o'clock. Draped in a black toga, he walked towards the sea. He stood looking south and although unable to distinguish it, Armorica lay straight ahead. Such thought gave him strength. In a short time, he would unleash his people on a country populated by natives similar to his own. It brought a shiver to his spine. The Saxons had caused the Celts to retreat and feel uncomfortable in their land. Instead of fighting a deadly combat where every inch would be battled fiercely to permanent demise, he had to lead his nation in a massive exodus. Konan felt his nation's survival was at stake. The die was cast, he would have the ultimate council. Doubts would be raised, but he knew how to alleviate them.

Chapter Fifteen

The expeditionary migration force was afloat and on course for the northern coast of Armorica.

The many vessels forming the armada had come from Braetoll, Penaravon, Gwenporz and Gwenaber; foot soldiers, chariots, cavalrymen, arms supplies, food stocks, and horses all sailed. The naval escort comprised fifty battleships, three hundred and twenty transport troop transport vessels, and eighty ships as supplied; the entire armada consisted over seventeen thousand warriors.

The flotilla headed for Aleth, with Konan, Poher and Efflam in the leading battleship. The speed was not fast but steady and deliberate. The plan was to have everybody ready twenty-four hours after the landing so they could defend or attack and be on the move. Supplies accompanied the advancing army while the ships returned to Domenea for just as many men and resources again.

Konan was pensive; his thoughts were not so much on the military expedition but on what would happen once they were master of the land. He had many meetings with Gralon about the topic. From all the intelligence gathered in the last few years, it seemed inevitable to push aside the natives if they did not want to share or cooperate. First, the Armorican armed forces had to be completely annihilated.

In less than two weeks, the Domenean forces had advanced south, west, and east and destroyed any Armorican resistance. They had killed as many as seven thousand indigenous soldiers, many wounded were murdered, and ten thousand prisoners were taken. The Britons had suffered only three hundred dead and eight hundred wounded. The only area spared was Landreger, the region where Konan's paternal grandmother was from. The civilian population of Armorica was also affected. Apart from relatives away from home to fight the invaders, a horrible toll was imposed on the women and children. The conquest was completed, in the military sense, rather promptly.

When a whole section of people decides to emigrate, their goal is to settle. In the Sixth Century, that meant putting down roots on land and working it. Konan and others envisioned one hundred thousand Domenean civilians would make the crossing; they had to be directed and allocated properties according to many criteria. Expropriation of the inhabitants of Armorica was to be avoided if viable. The new arrivals had to live alongside the autochthones. Theoretically, it was a noble concept, but the practicality was more intricate.

Each Armorican village and town produced a committee to negotiate with a Briton representative to decide how many newcomers could be assimilated in the social and economic reality of their region. Konan realised it was a delicate task with a race who had been occupied, subjugated, experienced hardship and even loss of family members, however, he thought it was the quickest way to show a true spirit of reconciliation and integration. These Armoricans were the same bloodline as the Britons—the language was mostly similar, the spiritual beliefs identical. Konan asked himself many times if he could have avoided the violence. One of the problems was the conquest had left a fair amount of widows and orphans. There was little chance the local females would have these "invaders" as a husband, lover, or father to their children. Strict orders were issued to leave the womenfolk alone. Economically, those women were stranded, they needed help. A solution was to link one of those families to a newly arrived group from Britain and live together in community.

Konan made Landreger his capital in Armorica. He convened a small meeting with his closest Briton compatriots.

'We have accomplished the first phase of our plan. Militarily, we have conquered the country. Unfortunately, the number of casualties and deaths to the natives has far exceeded that which we would have hoped. We need to live here, so do the Armoricans. We have to normalise the situation as quickly as possible. We may ask for the impossible because we want their friendship and cooperation but at the same time, we have ravaged their way of living. We, therefore, have to try to replace it with a new one, which will help them forget the past. To achieve this goal, we will have to produce efforts and creativity. We have started something, and the outcome was hard to predict. The responsible approach is to alleviate pains as swiftly as possible. We cannot forget we initiated that massive movement of the population because we felt for decades our freedom was being threatened. Now we are terrorising others.'

Konan paused for a moment to ensure all present were listening to his every word, then continued.

'The quickest method for blending the two populations may be to hold a joint fight. We are a new entity on this continent—some of our new neighbours will naturally feel anxious about us. We are the most powerful army in this part of the world, the most numerous by any measure. We should use it to explore and assert our new borders. The Armoricans have always had a problematic relationship with the rest of Romanised Gaul. They will feel a sense of pride, if not heart, to go and show their strength with a new waring partner.'

Fanch had been Cranadh's confidant, and although he was getting toward the sunset of his active life, his devotion to the country and its rulers were still intact.

'The conquest, emigration, or whatever we choose to call it, will cost us dearly. Armorica is not unified as we are in Domenea, and apart from the trading of the Venete and a few iron mines, the local economy is rather shallow. The conquest, in monetary terms, will not bring much to our coffers. It, therefore, makes it fundamentally sound to hang on to the tin mines of Kernow as long as possible. We have to govern two countries separated by water; that does not help.'

Konan agreed albeit emphasised the positive nature of the situation.

'What you say is correct. We have not simplified our tasks with this invasion, however, we have acquired living space; we can feed ourselves on both sides of the sea, and *that* is a valuable factor.'

'We have to decide shortly how many of us are going to stay in Domenea. If we become defenceless over there with rapidity, the Irish, Welsh and Saxons will invade without hesitation. If we are to be realistic, some of our people will never move but rather take their chances with the invaders. Others might emigrate to Cymru or Alba, and Cumbria may also see a flux of people from Kernow.'

'We have crossed the sea in avoidance of a fight to prevent extermination; defending Domenea would have been a war of attrition. It is ironic we have to impose our ways on people similar to us in many aspects, and in truth, they would have been better off if we had left them alone. We are inflicting on them what we feared the Saxons would do unto us. Let us convince the Armoricans we are now with them. We must tell them and prove to them we will mend the wounds, and together, we will secure the territory.'

'So Konan! We are ready to fight the Franks when we are emigrating here to avoid a long fight with the Saxons. Why cross the sea if it is to pick up another conflict with a group who are nothing to us?'

'Fanch, on the surface you are correct in your surmise. The Saxon aggressions have gone on for years; we know their determination, and strength that seems to surge as a tidal wave. They are barbaric, and with them, coexistence is not an option. With the Franks we shall be the aggressor. They have barely established themselves in Gaul. They are more preoccupied in soaking in the Gallo-Romanic governing culture. To test their western flank is an exercise to unite Celts of Armorica and Celts of Britain. Although Germanic, the Franks are not as fierce as the Saxons. Strange people... there are rumours they could be one of the lost tribes of Israel. Another advantage of moving east would be to take over the vineyards of the banks of the river flowing from the centre of Gaul. It could be an economic activity for us—regulate it and sell it to Eire and Alba, perhaps even the Saxons! Furthermore, slate quarries and clay from the south of the river could be used for building material and potteries.'

'You seem well advanced in your thoughts. When do you think you want to start planning that move?'

'Within the next six months. There is another project I wish to perform. I want to bring my attention to Cumbria which is somewhat isolated in our kingdom—in the north all by itself, it is vulnerable. Scots, Irish, Welsh, and Saxon, as well as those new invaders from the far north with their fast ships, are probably thinking of attacking an easy prey. I want to go over there and organise a massive exodus to bring these mountain-dwelling people into Armorica; they will be grateful for a more comfortable life.'

'Are you sure you need to go over there?'

'Yes, there is nothing like site reconnaissance to see things for real. I also need a bit of distance from all which is going on in my kingdom.'

Konan sailed back to Kernow where he asked his mother if she would accompany him to the land of the mountains and lakes; she accepted willingly.

The voyage was a seagoing expedition. Three boats, well-armed, sailed from the Cranadh estuary around Cymru and northeast towards the Cumbrian coast. On the third day, when the small flotilla had turned northeast, Konan, standing at the front of his ship, was in deep reflection and holding dialogue with his thoughts.

What am I doing moving most of my people from Domenea to Armorica? Only the soldiers, noblemen, and artisans will be able to follow. What is to become of the ordinary town dwellers? If they have a craft, they will be able to practice it and be in demand by the Saxons. Peasants will move in mass; the Armorican soil is better than Kernow. They will enjoy more security in a land not subject to Saxon invasions. However, those poor town dwellers, they have nowhere to go, and rumours rife of the genocide in the east of Britain causes me much discomfort. I have to reconcile myself with the fact I am responsible for the fate of any of my subjects, for good or bad.

Armorica is closer to the continental commercial hubs, and the people who will move there will have a better chance to survive economically. It makes me wonder why our ancestors move to Big Island in the first place.

Members of our clergy are going to emigrate as well, and they will be the cement keeping us together. I am also concerned about our relationship with the indigenous Armoricans. Those people have to be treated with respect and made equal to us but there will be abuses out of my control. Britons, landowners, noblemen, will all argue to get the same wealth over there and will try to cheat.

The swell was increasing, and the king went below to find refuge.

The three vessels finally reached their destination. The central city of Cumbria was Caerwick; a fortified city, it had been in a prolonged state of siege many times. The Picts had been trying to take it for years.

Darlon was the governor of Cumbria. He and Konan started talking at once about leaving the territory. They both thought a meeting with the Picts was a must. After all, it was by far a more sensible approach to negotiate instead of just abandoning Cumbria. The nearby

Picts would worry the Irish and therefore stop them from raiding the south west coast of Britain. The Picts would gain some land, but in return, they would have to treat the Cumbrian people fairly. Maybe it was a hopeful imagining.

The crowd assembled on the main square; many flags were flying. The people started chanting, *Dom-me-nea, Dom-me-nea, Kel-tia, Kel-tia, Ko-nan, Ko-nan.* Konan's eyes watered with a deep flood of emotions which overcame him. In his mind, he and these people were one. Then... it started like humming, intensified and developed into a full fervent sound. It was the most common hymn of the Britons of Big Island. It talked of how they came from a land far away and, through trial and tribulation, sailed to Big Island and formed a nation. It also mentioned the Curse of the Rhoem but how they had overcome it and reached the goals of which their ancestors had dreamed. By the end of the song, Konan's eyes were streaming with tears. He took a flag from the assembly, held it in his left hand and addressed the crowd.

'Cumbrians, you are the jewel of our kingdom. We are going to move you from your land, down into Kernow and on to Armorica. Although not having beautiful mountains, it has woods and good agricultural land as well as fishing water. The present inhabitants share our spiritual beliefs, and we will treat them as brothers. It is hard to leave your home, your land. The Scots, Irish and Picts have always been a threat, and we cannot guarantee your security any longer if you stay here. We are ourselves under enormous pressure in Kernow. In the tranquillity of Armorica, we will thrive. I do not have to remind you of our ancient ancestry; our traditions and customs go back a long way. We came from the centre of the old continent. *Never* have we lost our rituals and pride. Indeed, sometimes we have curtailed our pride to survive. So, brothers and sisters, I hope you will join me with the rest of the Domenean people in moving to Armorica. Long live Keltia!'

The speech left Konan drained. He asked Darlon to point him in a direction where he could ride towards the mountains; he wanted to soak in wilderness and solitude. He needed to listen to a stream tumbling down the hills, the screeching of a hawk, the noise of wild cattle.

Konan had been riding for about three hours when he reached a torrent; he decided to follow it up into a small canyon. At the turn of a stream, he was amazed and surprised to find a young blonde woman, bare-breasted, splashing her torso. He coughed to make his presence felt; she looked up and made no attempt to cover her beautiful chest. The sun and wind had coloured her skin reddish-brown. Her face was round, she had piercing blue eyes. Her hair seemed ginger and tied up with a headband. Her long skirt floated on the surface of the water.

'I hope I did not startle you. My name is Konan, and I am riding through the fells. I am amazed to find you by yourself so far from any hamlets. What is your name?'

'I have heard your horse for a while.'

'And yet you did not cover yourself.'

'Where are you from? Not from those parts I swear. I spend most of my time dressed in this fashion, when the weather permits it. My ancestors went about wearing even less than I do. Monks and religious people have influenced our habits.'

'Apart from bathing what brings you here, do you have a name?'

'I gather plants and stones; plants for health needs and stones for jewels. I go by the name of Theena. I am not from around here, but from the land above the Roman wall. I am one of the few Cumbrians who has learned to live and be tolerated by the Picts, Scots and Irish. Our language is different yet trying to survive in a harsh land brings us together out of necessity. They also appreciate the way we work iron and bronze.'

'What brings you down here?'

'There is a delegation of notables from my tribe coming to meet representatives from Cumbria, and the king of Domenea on a surprise visit. There are talks of massive migration from Cumbria to down south and further to another continent called Armorica. A pretty radical, severe and desperate act if you ask me. I would instead take my chances with the Picts. I don't know how one can expect someone to abandon their worthy possessions and the life they know to go on to a life of struggle and restart. Moreover, I like the landscape where I live, and it has a significant effect on me. Your accent indicates you are not from Cumbria either, where are you from?'

'Domenea.'

'Ha! You are supposed to encourage us to move.'

Konan paused as he tried to put himself in the position of people like Theena; they did not need to relocate. They were living with other ethnic groups, but they did not seem to mind. Maybe they were to be left alone.

'Where I am from, we do not have the luxury of living in peace with our neighbours. The Saxons are pushing us all the time, and it is better to prevent than remedy a situation when we would have to flee. Some of us are already in Armorica, and that is where we are going to regroup and settle. Theena, let me ask you... do you feel closer to us Britons or the Scots and Picts?'

'My ancestors make me close to you down south, but in my day-to-day living... I am closer to them.'

For the first time, Konan noticed her blue eyes and ginger hair. She did not resemble a typical Briton; she was fairer and full of freckles. She was not tall, but she had a beautiful chest and trim waistline. He could only imagine her legs were firm and muscular but still shaped in a pleasant way.

'Are you going to stay in the land of the Picts?'

'That is a difficult one to answer, my father is a Briton, and my mother a Scot. They have not yet decided to follow the great upheaval.'

'I would like to take a trip to your village and see its beauty for myself. Would you accede to my request?'

'I am not sure it would be proper to travel with a stranger. You seem to feel you have entitlement over people; there is an air of superiority about you. Are you a prominent landowner down south and in Armorica?'

'Yes and no.'

'I have heard you are invading Armorica, I expect the indigenous tribes are not pleased about having to negotiate, as you put it.

'I am related to them, I have many cousins, and my paternal grandmother is from Armorica. It is a beautiful country with a rocky coast, huge bays, thick forests, wild rivers and only three Roman roads. The Armoricans are our kin but instead of sailing to Britain a thousand years ago, they stayed there. They are Celts like us and conquered by the Romans. They took everything valuable from the Latins and rejected the rest. It can be difficult to see the difference between the Gauls and Romans; the Gauls speak a Celtic-Romano tongue yet in Armorica, the Roman influence was minimal despite doing commerce with each other, so they retained their language, which is similar to Welsh and ours. To the effect we can have regular communications when they agree with us, but they feign not to understand when they disagree. They welcome us to a certain extent because we are like blood brothers and together, we will be different from the rest of Gaul. Militarily and economically, it will increase their strength and ours.'

'But what is going to happen to the rest of Celtic Britain? Up here, we can survive—the Germans will never dare fight the Scots and the Picts, but are we going to abandon those who want to stay with these barbarians?'

'I am afraid those who decide to remain will have to suffer like a vanquished tribe. They will lose their language, their customs, they will be discriminated against, or they will organise themselves into a resistance movement. We will wait for and accommodate anybody who wants to follow us. You see, many people will want to take their chances. Theena, would it be possible for me to see where your tribe lives?'

'Sir, Konan, I do not think it would be proper to travel with you and bring you back but I can always ask my father.'

'You are right, it would not be proper. Many business matters are waiting for me down south. Do you want a ride back to Caerwick?'

Theena accepted Konan's offer. As they rode back, she held him by the waist; he felt a certain sexual feeling being braced that way. When they reached their destination, Theena dismounted. He had never put foot to earth when they were talking in the gill. He kissed her hand as they told each other that, maybe, they might see each other again in Armorica.

The encounter left Konan thinking about the prospect of moving an entire country. Was he forcing people to do it? It could be that regardless of race, custom, tradition, religion, family, people were attached by their hearts to the piece of earth they were tolling and living upon. That applied especially to folks having an intimate relationship with the soil, nature and farm animals.

A week later, Konan was back in Armorica. He attended a feast given in his honour by the family of his grandmother in the Landreger region. He deemed it critical to meet with Armoricans and try to extricate from their mind what they thought the influx of people from Kernow meant for them. Konan had it in him to make everybody content. He also knew it was impossible but would try anyway.

Konan was gladdened to have dinner with the closest people he could call family in Armorica. He was in the castle overlooking the river Jaudy. The tides had left their impression on the riverbed; at its lowest level, it unveiled the dirty undercoat full of oozing wrinkled mud.

Konan reflected what transpired at the occasion; his distant cousins were apprehensively polite at first. After all, he was a king of a great kingdom. However, as the meal progressed and the flowing wine gave the Armoricans bravado, they began voicing their concerns, reproaches, and warnings. They explained to Konan it was to be expected landowners, noblemen, even town dwelling people were filled with worries of losing something to the invaders who were fleeing their own land and their own troubles. They recognised there would likely be enough room for everybody but nevertheless, the Armoricans would organise themselves and would almost certainly protest and give fight for several years.

The military conquest had been completed; the results were far from clear. A territorial dispersion of the occupying army had followed the initial annihilation of any significant Armorican forces. Yet it was far from a complete victory as pockets of resistance were revealing their menacing heads everywhere. The Armoricans would keep their hostile spirit when facing an invader armed with the pretence of graciousness but in reality, brimmed with predatory objectives.

Konan was not surprised by what he heard but had hoped it would not come to this end. However, he realised he had stuffed away similar thoughts to a corner of his mind rather than face them.

Konan found himself speaking, as the meal went on, like the people of Landreger; he used their grammar, words, and idioms. The Armoricans spoke an archaic version of the Kernow Celtic mixed with Latin influence. Even so, it was still comprehensible to the Britons whose language had little changed since they had landed on Big Island.

The evening carried on—musical interludes, poetry recitals, and dancing were all performed.

Konan moved South with a with a small escort to the Gwened region. Several of the settlements were coastal garrisons such as Moraber, Landreger, Dol, Naonned, and Gwened. Inland strongholds were in Caerhix, Pontivy, and

Treveleg. The next goal was to land in the Odet river estuary and the Brest inlet. A line of forts was to be established on the fringe of Armorica, on land bordering the Frank territory.

The massive passage of civilians from Big Island was still six months away. The planning of the "move" was orchestrated in such a way it caused minimal disturbance and resentment among the local population. New lands were to be made fit for agriculture next to the existing villages so new arrivals could benefit from water sources and communication hubs. On the rare occasions where locals had to be forced into cohabitation with the Britons, violence was expected. The new arrivals hoped it would be the exception rather than the norm.

Chapter Sixteen

Initially the colonisation moved quickly and spread smoothly; the newcomers were well-armed soldiers, well behaved, and dwelling on the village outskirts. In towns where there was full-scale occupation, the relationship was tense between soldiers and city folks. However, the indigenous people were, in most cases, intent not to provoke any violent reactions—respect was born from fear.

In the midst of all this uncertainty, Konan returned to Kernow to find on arrival his mother had taken ill. She had developed a fever and had been in bed inside her quarters for four days. He went to see her at once—he could not understand how a physically active person could look so ravaged over such a short lapse of time. His presence cheered her up, and he started to sing, in Gaelic, some of the Irish melodies they had sung so many times since he was a young boy. His soul filled with sadness. His sixth sense told him something was wrong and a pain in his stomach signalled it was hopeless fighting it; destiny was doing its job.

Bridgit passed away too quickly; Konan did not even have time to discuss what her legacy should be. He knew in his heart what her bequest to him was: *Pride in adversity or glory*. There was no doubt in his mind she should be buried next to his father. However, he felt a part of her should be forever on Irish soil. He decided he would cut a flock of her hair, put it in a box and take it back to Enismon, her native village.

Knowing he would have to go back to Erin and risk being taken hostage, he took an armed escort with him. However risky, he owed it to his mother.

The box containing her hair was actually a rectangular container made from Domenean silver and coated inside with green velvet.

After a calm crossing, the three ships landed near Lahinch Bay. There were, all tolled, one hundred men of arms and some court people. One of them was Elenah, a long-time, Irish companion of Bridgit. They proceeded north, towards the cliffs of Moher. There, facing the westerly wind of the ocean, Konan took half the lock of hair and threw it in the air—it went up and dispersed itself inland. Like everything in Erin, the westerly winds from the Atlantic governed life inland. The rest of the lock was put back in the box and thrown down the cliffs where it smashed open, and the seawater scattered the rest of the hair; a part of Bridgit played a last tribute to the mighty sea whilst a priest recited an invocation. The party went back towards Lahinch hoping to remain unnoticed.

The road, from the cliff of Moher back to Lahinch and the embarkations, meandered on the plateau on top of the precipice then wandered down towards the plain of Enismon before roaming to the bay. As they were reaching the plain, suddenly hundreds of horsemen appeared, some armed with lances strapped on their backs. Elenah had not been seen since the Britons had started marching north. There was little doubt in Konan's mind his mother's confidant had harboured resentment for years and saw a way to avenge her murdered relatives of old. There was no way the Domeneans could avoid them. Konan made his horsemen charge the Irish left wing while trying to make a break for the seashore still a few miles away. It was then they noticed thick smoke originating from the ocean— there was no doubt their boats were on fire. It looked more like a trap every passing second.

Konan tried to manoeuvre his men toward the Irish right wing, but they anticipated the move and countered the king's men. The Britons were trying to stretch their opponents but to no avail. After a while, the islanders having watched patiently, moved in for the final thrust. Outnumbered three to one, the Britons did not have a chance, nevertheless, they put up a good fight. It dawned on them they were trapped so they might as well die fighting as it looked like the attackers were Hell-bent on taking no prisoners. The Irish had bet if the Britons disappeared, it could be attributed to loss at sea therefore avoiding any reprisals. After a while, only Konan and a handful of his men remained, with many Irish still standing.

Gelad, a bodyguard of Konan, slipped him some advice. 'My Lord, get rid of that golden chain and medallion, give it to me and I will wear it.' Gelad clearly understood the attackers would want Konan. What they might do, he was not sure, but it was not going to be pleasant. He hoped they would mistake him for the king— Gelad was ready to die for him if necessary.

The deadly encounter went on a short while longer; more Irishmen died, more Britons were slaughtered. At the end of the combat, there were five Britons left, Gelad and Konan among them, to the thirty Irish still standing. Proportionally, the Britons had killed more of their opponents.

Silence fell on the fighters. The Irish circled the five Britons. Cullohan, the chief, started to talk in a tongue the Britons could not comprehend; a few words sounded familiar, but that was all. Cullohan stared intensely at Gelad, observing the chain and medallion. His eyes settled on Konan, and he began to laugh, talking in Irish.

'That man is Bridgit's son, he looks so much like her. The other one with the gold chain around his neck is trying to pass for the king, and he nearly fooled me.' Cullohan lifted his sword and cut Gelad's skull so deeply, the bodyguard died as though stricken by a bolt of lightning.

Konan was seized, his hands tied behind his back. The three other Britons were killed by the sword soon after seizure of the king. A long rope was put loosely around Konan's neck and held by a horseman; he was forced to march to the beach where he landed a few hours ago. Thoughts dashed through Konan's mind—the expedition was a humiliating disaster and the price already paid for the risk he took was too high. But it was too late, too horribly late... he knew his fate was sealed. He felt empty and was not really aware of what was going on around him.

They finally reached the shore, Cullohan addressed his royal prisoner.

'Briton, did you know your mother was stolen from us, her people, and forced to marry your father, head of that inferior Celtic kingdom? Twenty of our chieftains drowned when they were taken hostage with her. You are to pay for these deeds, and I shall hold your head down in seawater twenty times.'

On first immersion, Konan felt his lungs exploding, his sinuses bursting with heat. His nose, throat, and ears were on fire. By the tenth dip, he passed out. His oppressors stopped and took him, unconscious, to their village where they tied him to a post and used his body as target in a bow-shooting contest. The first arrow struck his right knee, the next one, his left. Konan wanted to scream but his royal warrior resolve refused to allow such open emotion. The next dart punctured his stomach, the following his heart, causing death.

Cullohan felt vexed the suffering of his victim had not endured for longer.

Chapter Seventeen

With Konan's death, twelve hundred years of the Ervar bloodline came to a sudden end. The Irish had, in less than an hour, ended a family legacy dedicated to the continuity of mission to preserve the traditions of the Bryethi people. Cranadh, the great unifier, had brought pride to his nation and, seeing danger looming on the horizon, pushed the move to Armorica where he felt his people could continue living in a manner befitting of their values. Konan had faithfully wanted to advance towards that same path.

It took a while before the disappearance of the king and his escort was noticed. It took another month for every corner of the kingdom to know what had happened. Legends started; apparitions of Konan were numerous, and his bravery and deeds were accentuated to the status of mystical hero.

Domenea was ready to disintegrate; Konan's second cousin, Gralon, resumed leadership of the kingdom—governing had to continue. The emigration to Armorica had come to a stop. War against the Franks was an immediate threat and settlements were left without coordination and guidance.

On the borderland of Alba, near Cumbria, a blonde-haired woman took the news very poorly. She had met Konan in a gill in Cumbria, and their encounter had left an emotional impression upon her. Maybe she was a little in love with the man she had known for an hour or so. His humble manner had stricken her, and when she found out his true identity a few days later, she felt a mixture of shame and pride. She left her home and travelled to Kernow. Theena had time to think on Konan's words about the unity of the Celts, the Domenean traditions and the emigration to Armorica. She felt strongly that without him, the goals would not be accomplished. She did not know what could be done to continue the mission but recognised she had to be near the seat of power, and for that goal, she had to go to court to meet the person in charge. The undertaking was not an easy task. Her determination led to an audience with Gralon, who, impressed by her resolve, asked her to stay at court for a few days.

The meeting with Theena spurred Gralon to ask himself some searching questions about the future of Domenea. *Would being dominated by the Saxons be so bad?* The emigration was in its infancy and creating much incertitude. Gralon had the realisation he could not abandon the Britons already in Armorica. *How had a spirited woman from the northern edge of the kingdom seen all the facts so clearly?* Theena had only met Konan for an instant yet there was no doubt in her mind what the line of conduct should be.

Clarity struck Gralon; he would tour the kingdom to elicit who wanted to emigrate and who did not. He would make himself advocate for settling across the sea, but he wanted to evaluate the extent of the aspirations of the lords and their subjects. Another fact became evident to him. The succession to the bloodline had to be found; it had to be somebody who carried Cranadh's blood, however little it might be.

Cranadh's father, Ropaz, had a brother called Brennus. He had two sons, Gralon, the regent, and the younger Hewl who had passed away while relatively young. He had fathered a son, Sizum, who was now nineteen years old. That boy also had Irish blood in him. Hewl, having fought against Irish raiders in Eire, had taken, on a punitive expedition, a woman of noble blood who became his wife. Sizum was more intellectual than warrior, but he had fought during recent campaigns, and in Armorica. He had taken back to Domenea, a foreigner, an Armorican called Gaelb. She was from Treveleg and had met Sizum when he was stationed a while in a military encampment near the village. She was actually a descendant of Fanac; a hero in the eyes of the locals, a deserter in the eyes of the Britons.

Treveleg had seen tragic and violent events, and it had strained the relationships between Domeneans and Armoricans in the Gwened region—the village had witnessed troubles between immigrant soldiers and the natives. Fanac, a Domenean soldier, had killed his superior officer who himself had assassinated several locals including a resident Catholic priest. Fanac went on the run but it was rumoured he had blended in a village at a safe distance from Treveleg. He was reportedly working for a blacksmith, making metal weapons.

Gralon approached Sizum and explained to him the situation. Sizum felt he was not in line to take the title of chief of Domenea. However, he understood a head of state had to be appointed if the kingdom had any chance of survival.

The council of the realm's most important noblemen voted Sizum in. Those from Kernow knew him and felt it was not a time to argue or claim the throne. Those from the north followed suit without any objections or enthusiasm.

The circumstances remained and Sizum was crowned king a few weeks after the council's decision. Sizum's intellect was well above average and he was not a person inclined to take rash decision. He wanted to know the result of Gralon's survey to assert if the emigration to Armorica was supported. It turned out it was viewed as a must in Kernow and with many chiefs from Somerset. As far as Cumbria, their opinions were not so definite, and half of them did not want to move. The relationship with the border Scots was great, and it was fair to say they had lived harmoniously. Of course, the Picts further north were a constant menace, but it had been a while since they had endured their cruelty.

Sizum took notice of the intentions of the men in charge of his new kingdom and considered it his duty to continue the emigration. People from Kernow were to be the ones forming the main bulk of the move. He also wanted families to move with armed men. Within weeks, soldiers were sent to clear the space, and within months, a grass root movement from Kernow undertook the long sea voyage, rounding the west of Armorica; settling along the coast at first then making their way up to the interior following rivers.

It seemed a branch of the Celtic people had temporarily reached a turning point. The last twelve centuries had taken this corpus of a nation from what is now Bohemia to Western Europe onto the British Isles which they occupied with the exception of Scotland. They belonged to the Brythonic strain of the Celts and were present in Wales, the Lake District, most of what is now England and they had initiated their existence in Armorica, soon to be called Brittany (Little Britain).

At last, Sizum and the Domeneans had occupied Armorica.

Armoricans were Gaulish Celts; they had been invaded by people of the same blood, same beliefs, but the influx had nevertheless been a painful experience. The Armorican tongue was a mixture of Britonic and Gaulish, mixed with some Latin. The Romans had left a cultural heritage which was apparent in the architecture of some towns; they had built roads and forts, and introduced cultural understanding in sciences, philosophy, and literature. The Armorican elites were, at least in the urban centres, more sophisticated than the Britons. Their commercial acumen also made them superior to the invaders; they had long-standing mercantile relations with the southern and northeast ports of Europe. But the Romans never mixed blood with Armoricans, the latter were therefore of the same genes of their ancestors before the Roman conquest.

Sizum had passed away; his son, Artoad, was governing a good part of Brittany. The kingdom had two prongs—the northern coast as far east as Landreger, and the southwest of Brittany and around Gwened. A few spaces from the coast extended in between his jurisdiction. The interior was wild, and Sizum had given small vassals a free hand to pacify and govern it.

The eastern part of Brittany was made up of smaller chiefdoms where the rulers were descendants of people who had emigrated mostly from Cumbria. There were also several towns and adjacent lands which Irish and Welsh bishops or monks administered and created dioceses. Eastern Brittany was like a jigsaw puzzle with some arrangements from the kingdom of Artoad for military assistance if it was required.

The unity of Domenea on Big Island had not replicated itself in Armorica. The Armorican lords had become the vassals of the dominating Britons but nevertheless given the opportunity to contribute to the decisions regarding the ruling of Brittany.

To the east lay a big problem, namely the kingdom of the Franks. The Franks were initially from the region where the town of Frankfurt now stands. They claimed they were the lost tribe of Israel. Their emblem, the *Fleur de Lys*, had six branches, which according to historians is a reminder of the six points of the Star of David.

Armorica, then Brittany, was a territory the Franks looked upon with envy. It was a significant centre of commerce, linking south and north on the Atlantic coasts. The Franks also looked upon Brittany as a natural westward extension of their kingdom and expected the Bretons to become *their* vassals.

Artoad had raised an army comprising soldiers from all regions of Brittany but it happened the majority were from the east of Brittany. The Breton army was particularly cavalry-strong and a master of quick moves and clever formation and tactical changes. Archers, lancers, and sword fighters formed the infantry majority.

Once again, the Frank menace was raising concern, they were on the move towards Brittany. They were headed by Culperic, a Salian Frank whose kinfolk had fought with Clovis at the battle of Tolbiac and had decided the supremacy of the invaders over the remnants of Gaul.

Every time the Franks decided to take battle into Brittany, they would invariably use the same tactic. They would quickly get around Vitre or Fougeres and enter the thickly wooded area. However, there were not too many places they could come out, and the Bretons knew precisely where to wait for them.

A battle ensued in a location where Culperic's Frank forces occupied high ground; wooded enough to provide cover. The Bretons knew the Franks liked to charge on foot waving the famous "Francisque"; they were fierce close quarter fighters and would try to kill as many enemies as quickly as possible, retreat and try again. They would repeat this strategy this time and time again. The Bretons, on the other hand, were known for their swift cavalry moves. Artoad decided to have half his mounted troop on low ground at the bottom of the hill—the Franks would not resist attacking. The rest of the Breton cavalry and foot soldiers were ordered to go on a vast sweep towards the back of the Franks. Following the king's decision, the "Battle of the Hollow" commenced. The Celtic horsemen advanced in an elongated rectangle into the valley at the bottom of the hills; exposing their flanks widely. As expected, the Franks did not resist the attraction to attack. When they had nearly reached the southern side of the Breton column, the latter started to retreat swiftly westwards, that is to say from whence they came. The Franks having no more target to assault felt they might be trapped into an ambush and hence drew back towards the southern high ground, their starting vantage position. However, by then, the spot had been partially occupied by the Breton foot soldiers and the rest of the cavalry who had completed their long sweeping march. It was the Bretons' turn to descend on the retreating ascending Franks. The Celtic cavalry was at the same moment coming back to the fray and climbing the hill behind the Franks caught between two fighting factions. In less than half an hour, the Bretons had killed and wounded three-quarters of the enemy; Culperic was one of the dead. Artoad encircled a group of the foe and told them to go back to their king and convey the news it was not yet time for them to walk all over Brittany. Some of the Breton knights wanted to destroy the invaders, but Artoad felt it would carry a stronger meaning by letting them report what had happened; he had no illusion they would try again.

For the Franks, Brittany was an annoyance, but it was not as pressing to deal with as the strengthening of their burgeoning kingdom. Similarly, Artoad had to consolidate his realm and went back to Gwened. He went on a grand tour visiting various vassals to show his care for them and accentuate his army and government were there to help them. Artoad concentrated on showing a particular interest in the remnants of the old Armorican aristocracy. Even after the big waves of emigration, half of the population was still of Armorican stock. The two ethnic groups, being of Celtic blood, showed each other mutual respect, but there was no doubt the newcomers caused resentment among the invaded.

Chapter Eighteen

In the village of Treveleg, the majority of inhabitants were Armorican. One of the inhabitants, a man named Marthod, was given the nickname "Ar Brezonegh", "The Breton", a reference to the origin of his ancestors from Big Island. Marthod's father, Billig, was a brother of Sizum, therefore Marthod was a cousin of Artoad, and Gaelb was his aunt. Billig had married a woman from Gwened called Meire, mother of Marthod.

Gaelb, descendant of Fanac, spouse of Sizum, had ties with Treveleg. She had an affinity for her nephew and persuaded him to settle in the village.

Marthod, however, was not the type to settle, and for that reason, he boarded a ship carrying iron ore from mines near Gwened. He sailed to Ulster, then onto Fiona Island and his final destination, Alba. When Marthod disembarked, he had no idea what he was going to do. He left the ship and told the captain he would go back to Armorica someday but did not know when. For now, he was happy to discover a new land populated by people who were not speaking the same language but seemed to have the same daily preoccupations as his compatriots back in Armorica. He found a companion in a gentleman named Arch. They had met in the harbour. Looking lost, Arch saw somebody looking different and approached Marthod. They had a meal together, and Arch found out Marthod was looking for adventure.

Arch took Marthod on a journey traveling north into the deeper reaches of Alba. The Breton had never seen such landscape. There were huge hills mostly covered in green grass and rusty-coloured heather. Beautiful elongated lakes, which never seemed to end—the banks of these bodies of water were intricate hidden coves and wooded shores. It left Marthod with a deep feeling of how grandiose the earth could be. He found the area mysterious, mythical, and he thought only a Celt could fit perfectly within these surroundings. The tenebrous, complex, introspected Celts could thrive in this dark but imposing land.

As they were walking, Arch started to talk about who he was.

'You see Marthod, I am somewhat envious of you. You want to know why?'

'Yes why? Mind, it is reciprocal, I am must tell you I am envious of you also. I would like to live in your country with its beautiful scenery.'

'Well as beautiful as it is, sometimes I feel it has been stolen from me. We, the Picts, as far as we know, have always been on this land. There is no suggestion we have ever lived anywhere else; if we did, we do not know where it could have been. Then the Irish came... I have always wondered what made them move from Eire or was it just one of their tribes thrown out by their peers?

Regardless, they got a foothold, and we battled many times, and victories, as well as defeats, alternated on both sides. We tired of it and decided to tolerate each others' existence. Oddly, it is a reciprocal non-aggressive relationship. I believe the only thing that bounds us is the nature of the landscape. Occasionally we have surges of pride, and attack and pillage Scot settlements. Our spiritual leaders, who are similar to your druids, encourage such events. Our beliefs make us much more violent than the Celts. Our Gods fight therefore we fight.'

The two men carried on walking for days... for weeks. It was the end of autumn and snow started to cover the mountain tops. They finally reached a firth on the west coast. At the end of the nearly landlocked sea, there stood a massive mountain with a gigantic dome. Arch suggested they should walk around the southern side to reach the east face. In doing so, it took them half a day. When they reached the end of their march, they encountered the east facing rock wall. Nearly vertical and craggy with patches of ice, it looked hostile and imposing at the same time.

'Marthod', this mountain is the epitome of life; one side is smooth, the other one rugged. One is easy and uneventful to climb; the other is daunting and difficult. Most of us in life, because of our pride, will choose the most challenging route not even knowing or thinking if it is beyond our capabilities.'

The two travel companions retraced their footsteps using the same path. Going around the mountain would have taken too long and there was no clearly marked path. They made their way towards the west and reached a deep fjord. There a man, Arch knew him, stood next to a sailboat; two sailors were already on deck. After a few salutations, they all jumped aboard.

Marthod was going from surprise to astonishment; he felt he was discovering so many sights of beautiful landscape, and a feeling of joy, coupled with awe, overwhelmed him. It took the boat a full day to meander among the myriad of islands before they finally reached the open sea. Arch explained they were to sail to a big island to the west where ancient Celtic customs had been preserved for hundreds of years. Christianity, after many attempts, had never taken hold, so the distant past was very much present in day-to-day life. The island was actually two separate land masses separated by a strait; they moored on the one most northern.

The Pict and Armorican started walking north. They were met, after an hour-long walk, by a shepherd who took them for another two hours of trekking over hills in a northerly direction. They reached a village made of attractive well-constructed small houses; every dwelling had a sod roof. One could see there had been some planning in the way the small hamlet was laid out. At the centre, there was an open space with grass and a menhir [*men*: stone; *hir*: tall] as tall as two men. From here, a concentric row of houses formed circles, becoming larger as one moved further from the centre. All in all, there were fifty dwellings. The settlement was surrounded by grassland dotted with small rocky outcrops.

The village was home to a druid, Haliorch, who lived in the first circle. Tall, angular, long white hair falling below the shoulders, and a bald receding forehead; his frock was one long garment resembling a long robe. His tribe was of the strain issued from the Irish people, the Hybaers. They had sailed a century before to find an isolated island. They found it; Lewis was, in a way, the end of a long journey for those Celts. They had not forgotten the ancient rituals. They felt daily life in Ireland was inviting maledictions to fall steadily upon the Irish, they wanted to dissociate themselves and return to the rites of life as they were before they left their ancestral land, way back east.

At the time of the year the visit was taking place, the days were becoming slightly longer. Darkness was not growing any longer; brightness had started its journey. To thank the gods for the renewal of this phenomenon, a ceremony was in order. All the villagers were present. A huge fire burned in the middle of a field on top of a flat hill where a tall pole was stuck in the soil; everybody looked to it. The druid was talking to the gods; he would do so until sunrise. In the middle of the night, the people ran through the fire at such speed, the flames did not hurt them. Eventually the fire was allowed to die and when everything was completely dark, and every cinder watered down, a silence bore over the proceedings for hours. Finally, the upper portion of the sun appeared and rose until it was a full blinding circle—the right-hand side of the glowing orb was left of the pole whereas the day before, it was on the right. The sun, at last, had begun reversing its course... proof the gods had spared them and days would get longer from now on. The assembly voiced seven yells, they were cries of exaltation and relief.

Everybody returned to the village, Arch and Marthod were introduced to the druid. He took notice Marthod was a Breton[3].

[3]When the Domeneans emigrated to Armorica, the locals referred to them as *'Bretons'*.

'Are old rites still practiced in Armorica?'

'They are fading fast. We are in the process of rebuilding our nation on another soil and worshipping traditions are falling by the wayside.'

'It is important to stick to the traditions followed for thousands of years; failure to comply will unleash the furore of the gods. I do not have to remind you, the Bryethi tribes are in a precarious position due to the Curse of the Rhoem, a fact well known among us druids.'

A day later, the two friends started their journey south; they parted after a further week.

Marthod was back in Treveleg within three weeks. His journey had left him with a head full of souvenirs—spiritual feelings about the Celts of Alba and Britain—he had no doubt there was a link between all those tribes. A common trait was the landscape they lived in... it was rugged, not predestined to support human beings but they were grandiose.

After a short time in Treveleg, Marthod became restless once more. He had been told a war with the Franks was imminent, so he decided to enrol in the army. He became a foot soldier, armed with sword and lance. King Artoad commanded the army, but he had no idea his cousin, Marthod, had enrolled.

Chapter Nineteen

The Bretons pushed eastwards, they crossed the Loire river and shifted to a south-easterly direction. The terrain was wooded and became hillier, the height of the mounts higher and higher. They finally reached a region of cone-shaped mountains; these were the ancient volcanoes in the Arverni territory. The Breton warlords chose to visit these Celts who had, six hundred years earlier, stopped, at least for a while, the Romans. The Bretons were curious to see if any flame of Celtic pride still burned in their hearts. After all, Vercingetorix, the legendary hero, had made a significant show of courage at Gergovia against the Romans. If there was any will to fight and connect with the spirits of their forebears, they could join the Breton ranks and be a formidable force against the Franks. The Arverni were not politically inclined in waging any battle, however, a few hundred men did join the visiting army. Their military training was an enigma, but the Celtic command decided to keep them together and mould them into a fighting unit.

The Franks knew there was an army of Bretons on the move but were kind of puzzled by their whereabouts.

The Celts proceeded to march north. They went as far as Autricum which used to be a holy site for the Celts. It was like a belated pilgrimage of one thousand years. By then, the Franks were well aware of the twenty thousand-strong Breton army's whereabouts. They did not have as many armed men needed to engage the enemy. A mobilisation would have taken time; the Bretons were not aware of the Frank dilemma and overestimated the Frank strength. The foes did not want to battle each other since both felt they were at a disadvantage.

The Breton command was pondering on the purpose of the whole campaign. They had set out to tackle the Franks; however, it turned out to be nebulous. They wanted to test the integrity of their army made up of Breton, Armorican, and Averni. It was supposed to bind a common purpose for the three groups. A month and a half traveling in ancient Gaul was turning into pointless wandering; half of the soldiers had farms or smallholdings and wanted to go home.

A worthwhile goal was becoming requisite, and the chiefs thought of heading towards the land of the Normen, which occupied the north east shores of the sea, linking the continent with Big Island. A few easy battles would be the recipe for forging cohesion, in turn, good for morale. The landscape of the Viking or Normen territory was similar to Armorica; wooded and hilly. The main difference being, it was chequered with cultivated fields; the predominant activity was agricultural.

Artoad's army came in front of a sizeable castle; the gates wide open. The Bretons sent a delegation inside to notify the local lord the Bretons intended to set up camp outside the fortification. In addition, several crews would be harboured within the walls, and they expected to be provided with food comprising meat, poultry, vegetables, and water and beer or cider. The resident nobleman, a real Viking who had become an earthy aristocrat, was in no mind to start hostilities and therefore obliged the occupying force. The Celts staying inside the castle reported the inhabitants were unhappy about the manner in which the lord treated and oppressed them. They were Gauls who had become subjects of the Vikings. Artoad saw this unrest as an opportunity to take over the fortress and did so in the middle of the night after a few fights with the small garrison. The lord was chained down in a turret. It certainly made it easier for the Bretons to take whatever they needed, but the orders were to show consideration to the common folk. Nevertheless, some pillage and rape did occur, and the perpetrators were put to death promptly. Armies usually survived from plundering, however on this occasion, it was an order not to do so. The high command, having given the instruction, could not lose respect and therefore enforced punishment.

A council between Artoad and his generals took place; they questioned what they should do with this unexpected prize. *Should they leave and go back to Breizh?* The castle was not too far from the home border, so it was decided to leave a quarter of the force there while the rest returned to base quarters. All areas surrounding the fort had to be vested and administrated. One sizeable benefit was all the agricultural products that could be used. The way these local farmers worked could be copied back home and the production of dairy products was a specialty they could learn.

A small force stayed behind; Artoad led the rest back to Gwened. The long march was over; it had achieved the purpose of binding two peoples, the Armoricans, and the Bretons. The Averni went home to their land of ancients volcans.

Marthod went back to Treveleg but he did not stay there long enough to settle, he continued to travel across the Celtic world; it was a powerful draw. He came to meet in Kernow, a woman called Bodece who had ties on both side of the Breton Sea. From her family inheritance, Bodece, was land-rich on both sides of the sea. The situation suited both of them as they would commute often between the two countries. They never married but their bond produced a son they named Gerdan whose lineage persisted through centuries.

Chapter Twenty

Artoad was internally conflicted—*should he bind his people through armed conflict with powerful neighbours or should he concentrate on the well-being of the citizens of this relatively new country?* He took the decision to build a nation strong on commerce, agriculture, and robust institutions, with a universal religion. His armed forces had to be powerful but not seek out permanent conflict. A strong navy was essential for defence and safety of maritime commerce. Culture was a thorny subject; the insular Bretons were more rooted in the old Celtic traditions and had their own peculiar method of ministry inspired by Welsh and Irish monks. The Armoricans followed Gallo-Romano influences and a stronger tie to the pope. Surprisingly, Armoricans and Bretons were both attached to the druidic heritage.

Artoad felt his life was unravelling in slow motion. His aspirations of unity, prosperity, peace, and building a solid foundation were always put on hold by more pressing short-term concerns. Now, he sensed, was the right moment to concentrate on *his* tasks. Before he could do this, he wanted to reflect on his own life—he needed to know who Artoad was.

Artoad was born in Brittany, but he felt like a noble immigrant. The course of his life was similar to the one his ancestors had experienced on the other side of the sea. His rank isolated him, moreover an unwillingness to get out of the own circle to see what lay beyond. Artoad reasoned his caste felt that way because in their mind they were still in Domenea even after decades of being in Armorica... he had to become an Armorican or something close to it. He decided the first step was to espouse their language; not vastly different from his own, it was more like adopting the local dialect. The second step was to make the Armorican and Domenean faction feel like one. *Two motherlands, one sea, one nation...* he thought it a fitting precept.

For the transplanted Domenean—the farmer, the soldier, the merchant, the landlord—there would be no easy way to achieve what the king wanted, the will to change was not there. They thought they were the top strata so realistically it could take a generation to change. For the Armoricans, the incoming of their Celtic brothers from across the sea brought mixed feeling. On the one hand they welcomed the return to their Celtic roots, which had been eroded by the Gallo–Romano influence. On the other, they felt with no uncertainty they had been partially robbed of land and privileges. Instead of taking violent action, many had cleverly decided to infiltrate the newcomers' legislative and governmental apparatus, especially in the collection of taxes as it permitted them to keep a feel on the taxable mass of inhabitants and the philosophy of the people who raised them. They made suggestions that helped prevent the king and his administration from making unpleasant mistakes.

Artoad was in charge of a kingdom that could feed itself thus mineral extraction was not as important as in Kernow but significant nevertheless. Lead, tin, copper, and iron were extractable; marine salt was notable and strategic. Dioceses were the centres of culture and learning. Dol, Naoned, Gwened, Landreger, Kemper, St Pol, and Raoned were full of individuals with erudite capabilities. In many facets of life, the Bretons from the great island were important, but they started to blend with the economic intelligence of the Armoricans who had not been shy to borrow from the teachings of the Gallo-Romano knowledge.

Armorica's most valuable asset was its coastline with its estuaries and many inlets, which were natural harbours. Because of its ports and navy, Armorica had, for a long time, been the place of exchange between Southern and Northern Europe, giving it commercial importance. Artoad was adamant a military navy should be built to protect his merchant fleet; it had to be more powerful than the Frank, Saxon and Irish. The navy had to rival the Scandinavian and Northern Germans, these were the leading competitors, and Brittany would have to be the powerful military and mercantile force on the western Atlantic coast. The North Sea area would be an unknown quantity. Breton and Armorican seamen, to Artoad's mind, had to become the recognised experts in seafaring and commerce. Prosperity and diversification of resources were dependent on the sea.

The land itself, given its geographic morphology, was not auspicious for significant territorial ownership. The lairds wielded little power and their peasants, subjects, and workers were easily approachable. As consequence, the noblemen were aware of population perceptions and needs, thus the gentry was less oppressive than in other parts of Europe.

Artoad made it his duty to give back to the Armoricans, lands, forts, castles, and farms whenever death or legal situation came about; such action went a long way to bring back the self-esteem and importance of the native population.

The capital of Artoad's kingdom was Gwended. At the end of a large inlet, which they called the Mor Bihan, "the Little Sea", it was a natural harbour and easily accessible to the west and Kemper, and the east and Naoned and the Loire estuary. Artoad made a point to have subsidiary centres in Caerhey, Dol, Landreger, and Vitre. North-south communications were to be improved, and the Roman network was an excellent base on which to build. The granitic massifs were the natural source of road building materials; the interior still held a mystical aura and there was no doubt in the minds of most, the Celtic deities lived there. Predictably, crossing the inner region brought apprehension and fear. Hearty, tough people populated the villages established in that area; each of these entities had their own distinct customs and were disinclined to communicate with the outside world.

Artoad thought it a good idea to get these communities involved in the construction of the road arteries. Some could quarry the material; others could transport it. The primary objective was to connect all the villages, hamlets, and boroughs. In the course of the construction, it was inevitable people who were not aware of each others' existence would come to associate. Artoad required the planners include just as many Armoricans as Bretons. The structure of Brittany had to be created and what better approach than building something in the common good for all. Treveleg was not on one of the highways but as word got around, some of its youth moved away to labour on the undertaking. Artoad anticipated ten years for the length of works. Most of the roads were in a north-south direction and labour started on both extremities at once. The east-west communication veins already existed to a small degree but were non-existent in the centre of the eastern borders, giving a natural line of defence. The Loire River was a logical link. On the northern side, it was relatively easy to go into Normandy.

There was a general feeling all these structural works were positive steps towards progress and helped to strengthen the fragile coexistence of the old inhabitants to those relatively new. Artoad's vision to see a unified country was slowly progressing; for him, it was a moral obligation.

Apart from the tax collectors, army, clergy, and the various degrees of noblemen, there was no real organisation in the administrative machine. Artoad needed to know what was happening... what the people were thinking. He created a new class of administrators whose duties were to inspect and report the conditions of the structures, the agricultural activities, the relationships between lords and the lower classes, and in the towns, mercantile endeavours were monitored. These administrators were posted in every major city, every diocese and in the domains of the principal landowners. The officials recommended the representatives of the various regions to stand in an assembly in Gwened, where they were presented with significant reforms and laws conceived by the king and his council.

There were about four hundred members—noblemen, merchants, men of law, clergy and educators were present. The lower classes, such as manual workers and sailors, were absent. Any rejected laws and edicts were followed by a discussion between the king, his council and a committee of the chamber of representatives; compromise was usually reached between the three entities. This was a system of government that served the king well. He had adequate awareness of what was going on, and what he wanted for the country was at least communicated and reviewed by a diverse blend of his subjects. Compared with most realms of its time, Brittany was a democratic monarchy. Nevertheless, Artoad's representative approach did not satisfy everybody. The very fact he was the king of a thriving country created envies and enemies from within and outside the kingdom.

Brittany matured as a country. Kings succeeded and institutions became rooted. The condition of the ordinary people compared advantageously with the kingdoms of the time.

Relations with France were always tense and delicate. There had been numerous marriages between patricians of both countries, but it had not led to any rapprochement.

Normandy, next door to the east, was a peaceful neighbour. Both countries were foreigners on the soil of what had been Gaul. The Normans were Vikings from the north of Europe, but the Bretons were coming back to a part of the continent their ancestors had left centuries ago, but they were nevertheless considered outsiders. The language of the Bretons kept them apart; even the Vikings had adopted the Latin-based language of France. A frustration for the Franks and Carolingians was the fact those people, having come from an island, had successfully implanted themselves in a land utterly unknown to them, taken it over, and prospered; the whole process had been done with relatively no violence. On the other hand, the Franks and their descendants had to fight for every aspect of their conquest. The people of what had been Gaul had acquired the sophistication of the Romans and converted with some pains to their language. Having settled for one invader, it was excruciating for them to have to submit to these barbarians.

Artoad had been a predominant ruler in the Gwened region as well as in the east of Brittany. However, his grip on Breton Cornwall, the Poher and Dol areas had been limited, and the local chiefs did not recognise Artoad's suzerainty by their reluctance to send the levies Artoad's administration required. The king's envoys and inspectors frequently reported the difficulties of imposing the royal decrees on these vassals.

Artoad travelled in various lands of the Celtic nations. On one of his trips, he met an Irish maiden, Sieban, from the land of Ulster; she was thought to be a descendant of the legendary Cu'Chulain, a semi-mythical human being whose feats bordered reality and pure fabrication of the Gaelic minds. The couple had one son, Dann; the young man was not interested in continuing to deal with the legacy of his kin. His education was twofold; his father tried to get him involved in the affairs of the state but the young man was not interested. His mother gave him a taste for everything Irish. The contradictions in his mind resulted in Dann's passion for sailing the seas coming to fruition. On one of his voyages to the Norse countries he brought home Hildana, daughter of a Viking warlord. Their progenies insured the lineage continued for an extended period without interruption.

Chapter Twenty-One

Dann's reign took place in the Seventh Century. For two hundred years, Brittany survived numerous attacks from the Franks. The clergy asserted its power by creating numerous monasteries and parishes. The artisans of the religious map which was being created were mostly from Big Island and Erin.

Domenea had been a unified kingdom with a succession of supreme rulers. The immigration and conquest of Armorica had been achieved in sporadic moves and diverse tribes settled in places where they would find no jurisdiction. The new arrivals might had been vassals on Big Island but saw the chance of establishing themselves in a new country as an opportunity to be independent and not recognize any suzerainty from the descendants of Dann. The lack of unity made the territories easy pray for foe.

Brittany had to wait for Nominoë—a ruler who had the power to subjugate all the chiefs, including the descendants of Artoad and Dann. The dynasty of Domenea in Britain, which could trace its lineage to Ervar, who had left the ancestral homeland in the centre of Europe, had irreversibly run its course.

Nominoë's son and successor, Erispoë, was from the Poher[4]; ties to Domenea was as vassal of the Cranadh dynasty. The House of Poher comprised initially lesser lairds from the west coast of Kernow; that they were not prevailing eventually played in their favour. When they determined to make a push for supremacy of Armorica in its entirety, their relative political obscurity played to their benefit.

The new Poher stock carried on waging war with the Franks as well as trying to keep the Vikings at bay for a century. Brittany used its geographic location to improve its commerce with southern and northern Europe—ancient Britain was now a Saxon realm, but ex-foes had learned to be trading partners. The Breton navy was one of the strongest in northern Europe, only the Scandinavians could match it.

The Poher lineage persisted. Three centuries later, a young man, Trestan, inherited the ancestral land in Treveleg. The domain was modest; for what had been one of the most powerful Breton dynasties, it had only managed to preserve a comparative smallholding. Trestan was of middle stature with square shoulders. His face had high cheekbones and his green eyes contrasted with his black hair. He did not deem himself attractive and therefore had no clue how alluring he was to females. His life was spent administrating his domain. He was keen on making sure his subjects followed the laws but were also protected by them.

[4]Region of modern Carhaix.

Trestan knew the history of his family and was fascinated by it. Big Isle was a land of mystical preoccupation. He was yearning, one day, to visit and see where his distant ancestors lived.

There were rumours the kingdom of Normandy, to the east, had approached several Breton noblemen to ask if they would be interested in taking part in an armed expedition across the sea. Fighting the Saxons and the rewards of some land in Britain were proffered as incentive to regain what the Saxons had taken away from them.

Trestan was sensitive about his life's meaning. Looking at the achievements of his first twenty-five years, he saw a laird administrating a set of small towns and hamlets. His manor, near Treveleg, was modest. The welfare of his subjects was of importance to him, but only in so far as having a good conscience about his treatment of them. His notion of fairness as a lord to his servile people was skewed; hierarchy was to be respected, not questioned.

In Trestan's mind, the nebulous concept of going back to Britain was a feeling of revenge towards the Saxons; it was emotionally appealing. He knew the history of his lineage, and because of it, he felt this opportunity was unprecedented good fortune. It was also a way to get out, at least for a while, of his present situation which he deemed somewhat beneath his calling.

Trestan was a free man and the vassal of nobody. That made him relatively uninhibited to act as he wished as long as he did not upset anybody. To meet with the Normans in order to follow them into the invasion of Britain was a difficult undertaking, as he had no idea how to approach the relevant persons. One of his friends, Gavain, had mentioned to him the notion of joining the

Normans. Gavain told Trestan to go to Felger to make initial contact with the Count of Coutances, whose Viking family name was Lasse Haadjard; while Norman, he came from a long line of Norseman. Coutances was a close friend of Guillaume, Duke of Normandy.

Trestan decided to take the trip to Felger. The town was unique due to its role as a border town that had to fortify itself against intrusions from Normans and Franks. It was also a centre of commercial exchange and for that reason, was quite a prosperous and independent metropolis, and a natural link between Brittany and Normandy.

Trestan had to consider the financial implications of going to war. He managed his fiefdom in a thrifty manner; he had very few men of arms and each year the funds he save running all the estate was meagre. Nevertheless, he could leave a trusted individual to overseer everything, and take two men as companion soldiers. The three of them had to be fully fitted—horses, weapons, and armour. Trestan was versed in sword and combat lance, but his strength lay in his being a gifted rider.

Trestan met Coutances—it was a fact-finding quest for him, and an occasion for Coutances to judge if the Breton had warrior promise. The Norman pointed out, in bringing so few men of arms, it would be a challenge to get permission to integrate the army. In haste, Trestan said he could bring two-dozen soldiers with him. At the back of his mind, he thought it would take considerable persuasion to round up this many Breton conscripts. Trestan was given four months. A date and meeting place were agreed in the case of an affirmative answer from the Duke of Normandy. In the meantime, Coutances would let Gavain know within a week.

A week passed, and as a favour to Gavain, Coutances convinced the duke to admit the Breton join the invasion of Britain. More specifically, Trestan would join the Breton Army to fight across the Channel.

The Breton Army was to be an independent army corps, fighting as an entirely separate entity. Many details and procedures had to be worked out as they were an amalgamation of small detachments who had never fought together, even less as a single unit under foreign command. The task of the Normans was to evaluate, unite, and teach them how to wage war in the "Norman" way. They knew the Bretons had certain qualities, especially their speed of manoeuvrability.

Little by little, every Celtic tribe, groups of small fiefs, from noblemen to simple soldiers were all assembled in a camp near Bareuth. Language was a problem; only ten percent understood Gallo-Frank, fifty-five percent only understood Breton and the remaining thirty-five were bilingual. Moreover, out of all the linguistic groups, twenty percent implicitly spoke liturgical Latin. The Normans, on the other hand, were fully versatile in Gallo-Frank; very few still spoke Norse.

Trestan was an insignificant participant, dwarfed in the crowd of his Celtic brothers. His patrician rank made him, by principle, in charge of a small squad of twenty cavaliers he had recruited from Treveleg. His horsemanship, being superior to his subordinates, made him a natural chief but he still had to learn the art of war.

A more significant group was created and taught Norman tactics. The Breton commander in chief was a Poher. It did not escape Trestan, the family of his leader was junior, in terms of status, to his family in the past but they, with the twist of history, had become predominant in recent times.

Several months elapsed. The Bretons were improving their skills, but more importantly, their sense of pride and unity made them a disciplined body. They were not technically ready, but they made it up with dedication and purpose. Rumours were rife they would move to the seashore, near St. Valery, to practice boarding and lending of ships.

The moment proving the rumours correct finally arrived; the sandy shoreline was dotted with numerous boats, horses, oxen, chariots, supply wagons, and tents of all colours floating many pennants. For several weeks, at least twice a day they boarded the ships, went on the open sea and practiced landing on shore. Invariably they got soaked to the bones, and the rehearsals proceeded without full armour.

The important day came when animals and men practiced in full gear. The full operation became cumbersome with every move, the weight of the armour and weapons was dragging men and animals under the waves. Many soldiers perished; lessons of the debacle were learned, and the command felt it a blessing it happened during a mock-up.

Trestan started to realise this expedition idea was dangerous and life-threatening. From then on, he began to have deep introspection on several subjects. *What will I do in the scheme of this great endeavour? What will my behaviour be in combat? Are my motives realistic or too idealistic?* To all these questions, regardless of the answers, he knew there was no turning back.

Chapter Twenty-Two

Guillaume, Duke of Normandy, had no doubt in his mind he had a genuine legal claim to the throne of England. His ambition led him to mount the invasion of England in 1066. To this day, no other invasion of the island has been successful.

At the end of September, the amphibious expedition was underway. The crossing took a full day and a half after negotiating winds and currents. The landing area was a pebble beach, which transformed itself into a full campaign base camp. The commandants wanted everybody and everything on shore—units organised before moving inland. Several small incursions took place to familiarise themselves with the surrounding countryside. Destruction of properties also took place.

The time delay made several participants think it would wipe out the element of surprise. Guillaume only started moving when his scouts found out the Saxons were on the move to meet them, but they were still at a safe distance.

In mid-October the Norman army moved in a north-easterly direction and came to a pause at the bottom of a hill called Senlac. There they saw the Saxons were positioned on the strategically advantageous high ground.

Early morning, the Normans were ready for attack. The archers threw volley after volley of arrows, most of which landed upon huge Saxons shields. The Bretons on the left flank were the first to move uphill. Trestan could only hear the rattling of armour—swords and lances bumping into each other, the horses moving slightly, producing a soft metallic noise. Many thoughts and fears bordering on panic went through his mind. For a brief instant, he felt he would give anything not to be there. Sweat, hot at first then cold, rolled down his forehead and neck. It was a moment of reckoning... he thought he had made a huge mistake, there was no way out, and he was going to die because of his own stupidity for having decided to follow the Normans. His body weakened and he felt faint. His throat was parched, he started trembling and realised if he did not control it, his armour and weaponry would emit a clanging jingle. He managed to stop the shaking by holding his sword as tightly as he could. It crossed his mind, if at that very moment he were in the middle of a mêlée, in the thick of combat, he would not have the force to lift it. That precise notion made him realise he was not giving himself any chance of staying alive. His mind reacted; he looked around and watched his men, his companions, who were probably experiencing the same plight. He got some comfort out of that thought, osmosis of fear bizarrely from his men, probably as scared as he was, somehow gave him a passion for life. He made up his mind to be resolute and when the order came to advance, he would lead his men. He sensed he was a condemned man, but his life seemed less important than those of the sixteen Bretons in his squad. The order to move was to come as a death sentence.

Noise grew tremendously, shouting and horns announced the start of the fight. All the Breton columns moved forward and gathered speed. Halfway up the hill, a rain of arrows fell vertically upon them. Horses tumbled; arrows pierced bodies through armour. It was a rough awakening and fraught with excruciating pain. The Saxons, seeing the hesitation produced by their archers, decided to run toward the Celts. To the Bretons, the attacking force seemed enormous. They came to a standstill and without the order of retreat, they started turning back down the slope. Those who hesitated were butchered which only added to the panic of most who went back to the position they held before the start of hostilities. They were of no use as an attacking force.

As far as Trestan could see, he had escaped unhurt, all his Cavaliers were still standing on their mounts. The Norman generals took notice. That they had sent the Bretons to slaughter did not give them any due concern. But they realised by feigning upward sallies and then retreating downslope, they could lure the Saxons.

The "pendulum" move got repeated time and time again. The Saxons did not realise fast enough this was the tactic which would seal their defeat. When the Normans felt the enemy's numbers had petered out, they showered the hill with arrows—King Harold, the Saxon king, was mortally wounded. Then the Norman army in its entirety moved for the final slaughter.

By evening, every significant fight had ceased. Some of the Saxons were escaping in small groups toward the north; these fugitives were actively pursued and exterminated. The Norman reasoning was the more Saxons they could annihilate in the present, the less they would have to worry about in the near future. On the actual battlefield, the carnage had been substantial; three-quarters of the Saxons had been killed or were near death. Half of these events occurred in the last hour of the primary battle. The fierce fight they had put up faded toward the end of the day, and then their slaughter took place. On the Norman side, half the forces had either lost their lives or been injured. A high proportion of casualties took place at the beginning. Looking back on the successive assaults which made up the battle, which turned out victorious, one could not fail to see victory had been a delicate and unpredictable equilibrium between chance and skill, panic and courage. In the immediate aftermath, the Normans could mull over what had been the decisive action and at what moment it happened. The versatility of Guillaume and his lieutenants to realise their initial plan was not working and change to adapt to the situation was, for a neutral observer, what turned a potential disaster into a victory.

Methodically, the Norman soldiers killed and robbed the Saxon wounded, ignoring their cries for mercy. The captured weaponry was carefully sorted out. The Bretons lost only a quarter of their forces. Most of it happened during the initial upward surge which turned into a near debacle. Following that shocking moment, they had regrouped and taken an active part in the fight for the remainder of the day. They were motivated by their pride having been hurt by the morning sally and the necessity to redeem themselves. They were surprised by the savagery of the Normans, however, they did their fair share of pilfering.

Instead of joining in the dismal activities, Trestan attended to his horse, the animal looked exhausted. His men were also tired, fatigued and numb from the horror of warring. He was concerned, but none had been killed or injured. Emotions ran high inside their brains; the events of daytime had been so fast, violent, intense, and terrifying, they could not process it. In the space of a few hours, they had been immersed in situations none could have imagined—it was hard and depressing. Trestan felt a thick layer of sweat and dirt clinging to his skin. He needed to take off his armour and jump naked in a cool stream but with no running water nearby, he had no option but to wait. He could hear cavaliers shouting in the distance, finishing their sinister task. The awful sounds of the wounded, added to the moribund Saxons being slaughtered, hardly disturbed him; he did not know what emotions meant any longer for the blankness of spirit had settled on his persona. Sleep took over as he stood, even falling to the ground did not wake him.

Chapter Twenty-Three

The spoils of war were to come. Trestan expected the issue of rewards would be discussed sooner rather than later; the distribution of land in Britain for Breton noblemen, was after all, his drive to fight. He sincerely hoped he would not be the recipient of a meaningless title or standard loot. He wanted land property and to be a part of Big Island gentry; he felt this his due because of his ancestral lineage. Trestan also thought between Norman and Bretons, it would be a bitter dispute for the privileges.

Guillaume le Conquérant, the new king of England was the decider. Trestan's only ear to the king was the Duke of Coutances so he kept a close relation with Coutances and told him what he considered fair. The Breton wished for a piece of territory in Kernow, five hundred chains by five hundred chains with a small manor, good agricultural fields, and sparsely wooded with a running brook.

The Battle of Senlac, or Hastings, was only the beginning of the conquest—fighting continued in the months that followed. The Saxon gentry needed some persuasion, and the Normans had to force their way on manors and castles. Even after William was crowned King of England in London, the fights and skirmishes persisted. Trestan did not have to be swayed by Coutances to carry on serving the Norman cause; he and numerous Bretons went west and north on this pacifying undertaking.

Trestan came to like the countryside, it was quite similar to Brittany. He had not prepared for the hostility of the inhabitants, it depressed him and made him yearn to go home. He visited Kernow, the land of his ancestors; he tried hard to get close to the Celtic population but to no avail. The natives had either forgotten their origins or had been so assimilated in Saxon ways, they did not understand the foreigners who pretended to be their brethren. It marked Trestan, he did not comprehend this antipathy. He could not wait to go back to Armorica. However, it was out of the question, he had to wait for Guillaume to bestow the rewards upon the Breton knights.

Coutances finally told Trestan to go to the royal palace in London. Dozens of Breton nobility were assembled in a castle courtyard in the heart of London near the river. There, on a platform stood the conqueror of England. Each recipient was to step forward when his name was summoned. Trestan was so nervous his legs shook; he felt the same before the Battle of Senlac. Finally, his name came... Trestan of Treveleg, was to be given the title Lord of Rodmell, Guardian of the manor of Telscombe and keeper of the church of St Lawrence in the County of Sussex. In the same hamlet, he was also given the lordship of farms and agricultural acres near the manor. The word

"Sussex" went through him like a spear. Gone were the hopes of being granted territory in Kernow. At the same time, the acreage was quite sizeable, and curiosity took over his thoughts.

Trestan decided to look at his new holding with some of his men, hence a few days later they came upon a valley with a meandering river. The hamlet that bared the name of his title was on the west flank; he was anxious to get to the manor. After making enquiries, they were on their way to the crest line of the hills or "Downs" as they were called in that part of the world. They rode westward on the top, going west, until they saw a vale going south and there it was at the bottom, the manor, and quite close to it, a church with a square tower where St Lawrence stood.

The manor itself was built with chert; a local siliceous pebble found in bands within the chalky cliffs of the coastline. The bands, in their original environment, contrasted with their darkness amid the white of the chalk. The building was surrounded by a garden made up of grass and flower stems, which in full bloom, must have been a delight to the eyes. To enter the edifice, one had to pass through an arch and beyond it lay a squared courtyard. On the far side was the main hall. People started emerging from doors, about a dozen. They had apparently served the Saxon landlord, presumably killed at the Battle of Senlac. They had that look of apprehension and arrogance; they seemed anxious yet proud.

Verbal communication was a problem, the manor's inhabitants spoke only Saxon, and the newcomers French. The state of affairs was solved when the rector of St Lawrence appeared and conversed in Latin. From then on, the dialogue between the two groups went back and forth with the priest as an intermediary of the interactions. The Saxons said they were devoted to their departed lord. Trestan made a point to convey he was their laird and expected them to carry on looking after the estate. He also imparted keeping a certain fraction of what they produced and raised would be a reward for the fruits of their labour. He warned them the tax collector of the king of England would be visiting to do his duty. There was a garrison of Norman soldiers in Lewis and if they needed assistance to defend themselves, they could count on them. What was not said was the same soldiers would be used for repression in case of troubles initiated by the villagers. As far as what would be left after tax collection, it had to be given to a man of trust who would come every quarter; half for them, the rest for Trestan, whose share would be kept in a safe place in London. He explained his home was in Brittany and his ancestors reigned over England before the Saxons came. He would treat them fairly as long as they did not cheat him nor betray his trust but, if they did, he would deliver them to the Norman justice in Lewis.

The priest, Friar Cedric, showed Trestan the church. The new landlord had to sign a register with his name in Saxon, and list all his titles, Norman and Breton; doing so, he became the protector of St Lawrence Church in the village of Telscombe. St Lawrence was a martyr, believed to have been the guardian of the relic of the Chalice of the Last Supper, that is to say, the Holy Grail and all its mystical and magical power; Trestan thought this a great honour and particularly enticing.

At last, the Bretons considered resting from their long journey and the introduction parley which had been emotionally challenging and stressful. Following a meal, they were about to sleep, but for safety, one soldier stood guard. It was then the sentry told Trestan a man wanted to see him, and the fellow spoke a little Breton. It was the estate foreman, Mikelic. He claimed to be a descendant of the Celt who populated the region before the Saxons invaded, he also added his family never really mixed with the "intruders". He told Trestan he could be trusted to look after the estate.

Some days passed and Trestan was struggling with a dilemma. He was torn between staying longer in Telscombe to ensure the administration of the estate was well established, and travelling back to Traveleg; he missed his native land more than he anticipated. Conversely, he needed a trusted overseer. Mikelic's presence was fortuitous, but Trestan did not know him. He therefore asked if any of his men favoured being acting Lord of the Telscombe Estate and surrounding lands. Ralloch stepped forward; he was a level-headed landowner from the Gwened region who became a hardened warrior. He reminded Trestan his siblings administered his holdings in Brittany. He let it be known he wanted to seize the opportunity to manage a vast domain as long as he could rip a fair share of the fruit of his administration. Trestan saw that opportune proposal as a way out. The England campaign had been a long and exhausting venture; he was lucky to have come out of it alive. He could not help feeling disappointment. The dream to own land in Kernow had not materialised, other more powerful Breton noblemen had taken the best rewards. Gone were his objectives of getting back to the land of his Celtic ancestors and receive back from the Saxons what he felt was his legacy. In spite of this, his conscience had to accommodate the reality the Saxons had lived in Old Britain, now England, for three hundred years and he felt his claim was to something he no longer held right.

Three weeks later, Trestan was back in his domain in Traveleg; his people were pleased to see him. Such a long absence meant a great deal of catching up had to happen on a variety of matters. Recriminations and praises were in order. Trestan was not fully satisfied, despite the devotion of his servants and administrators. All in all, it was manageable anxiety.

Trestan was surprisingly restless, and an old vision of exploring other Celtic lands kept surfacing in his mind. Erin was specifically of interest to him; he knew he had some Irish blood in his veins. He started to think of a solution to sate his desire to travel. The idea of commerce entered his mind; if he could find products worthy of export from Brittany to other Celtic realms, it would satisfy his wants, but he could not find anything worthwhile to trade. After lengthy reflection, he deduced he would have to journey by himself to Cymru, Alba, Erin, and Kernow.

For the next two years, Trestan disappeared, leaving his Breton and English estates to trusted administrators. He imbued himself into the customs, history and particularities of the regions he visited. He often took jobs which were insignificant but made him stay close to the real life of the various nations. He asserted his rank on some occasions, on one of which he married a Welsh woman called Caerwynn; she was the daughter of a lesser nobleman from North West Cymru. He accepted her without a dowry. They spoke the same language or close enough to live together. She was younger than her husband, had beautiful red hair and piercing green eyes. Caerwynn was considered an intellectual, being well versed in Roman and Greek cultures, and encyclopaedic in Celtic matters.

The Welsh were of the same Celtic strain as the Bretons. Some Welsh had immigrated to Armorica. They had arrived in Big Island at the same time centuries ago. Some tribes settled in the mountainous and rocky lands northwest of Kernow and kept to themselves; Roman invasions hardly touched them at all. The geography of the country was definitely a factor which helped them weather incursions. They were subjected to a few Irish raids and occasional Scottish attacks They also used the help of the Vikings to fend off the Saxons. The Normans were more determined than ever to explore the possibilities of bringing them under their rule.

Chapter Twenty-Four

In moving to Gwened, Trestan hoped this mercantile centre would inspire him to establish a trading concern. He had gathered a fair amount of contacts in the Celtic world; Brittany was clearly the link between the southern and northern western fringes of Europe. Much commerce between Armorica and its Celtic brethren was usually specialised, involving a single type of merchandise. Trestan had the idea to trade a variety of goods—wine, cider, lace, textiles, fine swords, wheat, rye, some non-perishable vegetables, and jewellery, building materials such as roof slates, wood from Brittany and the Middle East. He believed if one product was not in demand, another one would be in favour. He journeyed to ask several of his contacts if they would be interested in buying his goods in bulk. He also secured warehousing for his merchandise, initially in five different places. He managed to convince the buyers they had to pay him half the order cost in advance and if any goods were damaged or perished in in transit, he would credit their accounts accordingly. Currency and ways of doing business differed in each location. It became obvious the complexity of the trading required a permanent agent in each location. For reason of trust, the agents had to be from Gwened. Couriers would travel back and forth to the various places to transmit orders. Trestan decided he would keep the proceeds in the five ports. Coins of gold and silver were accepted; the tenure of the metals would determine the value. He decided to encourage local tradesmen in the five regions to export their goods to Brittany or the continent of Europe. Wool and beer were the most important.

It took four years for Trestan's plan to became tangible. Trading increased at a steady pace and his wealth, although spread only in the Celtic fringe, was emerging as substantial. His achievements outstripped the power of what a lesser lord of Treveleg and Sussex could control. The five locations outside Breizh, the hubs of his mercantile empire, were Bristol, Southampton, Dublin, Oban, and Whitehaven. The eastern part of Scotland was strategically too far, although there was a fair amount of business to be done there.

Having all this money in the five locations, Trestan became a money lender to businesses and commercial ventures. He purchased domains with parkland, castles and manors. He probably held more land in the western fringe of the Celtic world than any other sole individual.

Although his trade directed him towards the north, Trestan could not find a better place than Gwened. A port on the northern coast of Breizh would have been ideal, but all the storage and imports from the south of the continent made it easier to be on the south coast. The main obstacle was the communications trough within Brittany. Very little had been done since the Romans had the vision of building a north-south axis.

Apart from running his trading empire, Trestan did not have much of a private life since he was utterly absorbed in the management of his business. Without realising, Trestan had sway within the western Celtic world. He had accumulated so much wealth in Brittany, Ireland, western England and Scotland, his position was unique; Trestan was like a king spreading his influence in the Atlantic fringe. His power was discreet and well dispersed. It was fitting his birth right had given him a diminishing legacy. With the help of the Normans, he has acquired land in England, however, what he had built over a few years was mightily impressive.

The "Bloodline" had not only survived but recreated itself. Trestan was controlling his own fate with remarkable effect. Through his commerce and sphere of influence, he had seen the characteristic traits of the western Celts. He was able, more than any other, to understand the diversity and unique needs of each Celtic nation. He was not fully conscious of the blending concept; he simply recognised the need to empathise with regional customs and be cautious to follow convention. In addition, he realised how narrow-minded some of the inhabitants could be; few grasped their common historical background or that their strength lay in alliances.

If there was a town where Trestan felt most at home, it was Whitehaven in Cumbria which was a forgotten Celtic region. The scenery of rounded mounts, hills and rocky crags, speckled with mythical and enigmatic lakes, touched his heart.

The more his enterprise expanded, the more Trestan had to pay attention to all angles. Fraud, paying and being paid on time, relations with buyers and suppliers—all this had to be done with the cooperation of trusted help. He created an elaborate system of supervision. The key was to make every separate regional administrator feel he had autonomy and a stake in the profits. Consequently, directives were delivered in a tactful manner and administrators conducted their business with professionalism.

Trestan was naturally skilled in anticipating his buyers' needs and matching them with his suppliers; he had a good sense of popular trends and what was falling out of interest. He played on all those factors to create needs in the merchandise he was selling, and raised or lowered prices accordingly.

Easy to predict, his mercantile activities did not stay unnoticed by the rulers of the lands where he conducted his business. He was meticulous and tried to remain inconspicuous but when he could not do so, he presented them with humility. He obliged them whenever possible and when unable, he provided explanation with the utmost tact. He knew only too well he could never appear too powerful; those rulers had the ability to get rid of him in countless ways therefore he played many cautious juggling acts. The Irish rulers were the most powerful in the sense there were few of them and they reigned over sizable territories. The Welsh were more significant in number and not necessarily affable to one another. The Scots were the same. The ruler of Cumbria was cordial and a humble, straight individual. Regardless of all those kings, dukes, counts and barons, Trestan held more power than any of them.

The Church bishops and other dignitaries also had to be handled with *velvet gloves*. Gifts were of custom; justified as a gift to God, not as bribe to His minions on Earth. Trestan laughed at corruption being a spiritual act when dealing with religious potentates.

Trestan had a stressful way of life; a reality he had to deal with. His constant travelling left him little time for seeking within himself for the meaning of his existence. Whenever activities quietened, he became depressed, unable to face being alone with his inaction. Instead of seeing those moments of relaxation as essential occasions to pause and rest, he suffered feelings of culpability about the little time he spent with his kinfolk. He found difficulty staying close to true friends or people with whom he could confer. Trestan was lonely, many times he concluded his own happiness had to come second to his enterprise. To his mind, it was of historical significance for it linked the Celts on the western fringe of Europe.

His marriage to lesser Welsh nobility, Caerwynn, was a convenient political act; his relationship with her was fair. When he was in Gwened, he made sure they spent considerable time together. They both enjoyed going to Cymru; her family was in awe of Trestan, and they were proud people who would not contemplate accepting any favours from the Breton. They lived near the highest mountain in the north west of the little kingdom.

They held relatively low status in Welsh gentry, their insularity was ingrained as well as amusing. They firmly believed the world revolved within the boundary of their land. The concept of a Celtic nation embracing the entire western fringe of Europe did not shake them emotionally; it never occurred to them identity had to be safeguarded, with force if necessary. The Welsh had fought for theirs and remained proudly independent. However, if the autonomy of other Celtic realms was threatened, they showed indifference and would be hard put upon to take up arms. Trestan thought they needed educating about the rest of the Celts. He mentioned, whenever he felt appropriate, the story of his family and of the Breton race in general. He was never sure if his teachings sunk on hollow ground, but he tried regardless.

Apart from Brittany, Trestan's favourite country was Cumbria. It had held links with Domenea for a long time but had become the forgotten member of the kingdom. He loved their land, and the rulers were affable, humble, and for most of them, trustworthy. He enjoyed staying in the manors of some lesser lairds in the hills. Rumour had it, Trestan was in an intimate relationship with the daughter of one of the lords. The discretion was so critical, it was hard to determine if there was any truth in the speculation, but the frequency of visits suggested the gossip carried some foundation.

Sheep and hill cattle were the principal export of Cumbria to the rest of Celtic trade; it was an unpretentious and steady commerce. As a whole, everything about Cumbria was subtle, yet beautiful, its people did not need to swank, their lives were contented and full of serene insurance.

In contrast, the relationship with Erin was anything but placid. The Gaelic Celts, son of Erin, had reached the island around the same time the Brythonic Celts reached their Big Island. They found the resident inhabitants even more superstitious than *they* were. The Hibernian, as they called themselves, were boisterous amongst themselves and had no affection for outsiders. In business, it was a job to keep their attention on any deals or get them to respect deadlines. They believed everything had to be done to their schedule. They were quick minded, and quick to quarrel. Reliability in business dealings was not a well understood concept. It is logical when the Vikings settled in relatively large number in Ireland, they found a people with similar views on many subjects. The Irish had been raiding their fellow Celts with impunity, but they found a match in the Vikings.

The Scots were closely related to the Irish as far as blood and language were concerned. The move to the northeast was likely started by monks in search of solitude but was soon followed by more secular people. Those settlers left behind the volatility and short view of life, and focused their energy on hard work, planning and a desire to lead a well-regimented existence. The climate being such in winter months prompted the necessity of saving for harder times to come. When they moved, they found the Picts who used to paint themselves blue when going into battle. The two blended rather well. Courage and ferocity were the contributions of the Picts, pondering before action was the gift of the Scots.

Trestan thought the landscape of Alba so dramatic that, at times, it was even frightening. The fog, which seemed to stick to the land did not make it any more pleasant. Although the Scots were tough to trade with, they were straightforward, and the Breton appreciated that.

Remnants of Trestan's people lay further south of Wales, they were the ones who had decided against resettling in Armorica. They had mixed with the newcomers, reluctantly with the Saxons first, then the Normans. They were similar to the Bretons but more taciturn. A practical people, they knew there was no sense in rebelling. Trading with Armorica gave them a natural open communication with the continent.

In a quiet and surreptitiousness way, Trestan had achieved a mercantile union with the western Celts. His trading network produced rapprochement among the nations, but was limited to the commercial classes only. If a Scot made a trade with a Welshman, it was about goods being exchanged for payment; never was it politically motivated nor viewed as a threat by the ruling classes. Trestan, having a long lineage of aristocratic blood, bridged the two universes, but being unique in his position, he was frustrated his vision had not advanced the concept of amalgamation within the Celts. Too many of these dukes, princes and kings were set on keeping the powers they had; rapport with other Celts, most of the time, was, alas, limited to the battlefield.

The more successful and involved Trestan became, the deeper his depression. What had started as a challenge was becoming a toil. He had a wife in Brittany and a mistress in Cumbria—the ambiguity of the circumstances troubled him, further exacerbated by him not having an heir. The situation on the continent was also of concern. The Plantagenet dynasty was spreading its insane influence, Brittany was becoming the object of rivalry between the Anjou-Aquitanians on one side and the King of France on the other. Constance Yof Brittany, by marriage, made the Angevin rulers in Brittany; a decisive moment as from then on, the Breton kingdom had rulers with diluted Celtic blood in their veins. Normans, Franks, and the House of Anjou governed Brittany... true independence died then.

Trestan was extremely despondent. He went through the motions of life without much enjoyment. Where others would have sunk into escapism such as alcohol, debauchery, long aimless trips, Trestan knew these would only serve to increase his sadness. Depression followed him from Cumbria to Brittany passing by Erin and Wales, it was with him on the seas, in the valleys and mountains. It was unshakable. His mind functioned as an automated machine, following a pattern and train of thought he could not control. Endangering his existence was a way in which to cope with his mental state so he sought physical activities and those involving substantial risk.

ꙮ ꙮ ꙮ

Trestan was on a sea voyage, making an inspection of his business conglomerate. Returning from Wales, his ship was sailing towards Landreger, on the north coast of Brittany. A moderate distance from the shoreline, shy of the estuary leading to the harbour, Trestan told the crew he intended to swim to the rocky shore and pick up clothes and horse from a farmer he knew. The captain thought it strange, but it was not the first time he had done a similar drill, however this time the swell was significant, and the currents were strong from east to west. Trestan stripped and dived into the dark green sea. The boat kept moving, and quickly his head and moving arms were nothing but a speck in the choppy water.

Three days later, Trestan's body was found on one of the numerous islands off the coast, west of Landreger.

Chapter Twenty-Five

Once again, the bloodline was interrupted. Trestan's sudden death left no heir for his union with Caerwynn had been childless. Ervar's lineage, which had left the ancestral land eighteen centuries previous, was in danger of ending. The dynasty was no longer sitting on a kingdom. In Brittany, the meagre Treveleg domain was all that was left from the glorious past.

The lineage of Sizum, Artoad, Dann and several generations, ending with Trestan, had run its course; it had persisted six centuries. A parallel heredity had stemmed. Back in the Sixth Century, Sizum had had a brother, Billig, who married Meire—they had a son, Marthod. Marthod travelled extensively, fighting the Franks. He never married but had a son, Gerdan, with a woman called Bodece. She was of impeccable pedigree from a long line of noblemen, some of whom had fought with Cranadh. Her family owned lands on both sides of the Channel, in Kernow and Brittany. Gerdan, albeit a bastard, was nevertheless wealthy through inheritance of his parents' estates, especially his mother's. Gerdan married Morgana, a young lady from a powerful Irish family. It was uncanny how matrimony with Irish maidens kept occurring through the history of the line of Ervar.

Twelve generations after Gerdan, roughly five hundred and fifty years forward, the inheritor of the lineage was a man called Padrig. The bloodline was persisting and was prosperous. Padrig inherited lands in Kernow and Brittany, Cumbria, Wales and Erin. He also became the owner of all Trestan had gathered, Treveleg, said to be the real fiefdom of the dynasty yet Padrig had no desire to live there. He preferred to reside in Erin; the high-spiritedness of the place stimulated him. He was particularly well read; he was more versed in the heroic acts of Cuculohan than Arthurian legend. Boisterous, he was at ease fighting skirmishes, mostly in Erin. The maternal bloodline was more relevant and respected in Erin; Padrig was considered one of the people, a man of Munster. When he was a boy, he spoke Breton at home, but with little effort made to speak it properly, the result was rather awful.

By the time Padrig reached his late teenage years, he should have been getting acquainted with his responsibilities as an important squire in England, Kernow, and Brittany, he was instead warring in chiefdom skirmishes across Erin.

Although Padrig tried to go out of his way to fit in, he always felt he was an oddity in Erin. The Irish believed and behaved as if they were the chosen people of the Celtic world, moreover, they truly felt no one else could ever count in the universe. Despite all this, life was pleasurable for the Breton transplant, and even with his wealth, he was treated on an equal footing. Being at the forefront of a small empire of commerce and property, he travelled often, but going back to green Erin was always a magnet and calming influence.

As an adult, Padrig improved his linguistic skills. He became well-versed in Gaelic, Breton, Welsh, French, and English. Latin had also been part of his education.

Short of being the sovereign of a realm, Padrig's power was second to none. He called for a gathering of all his domain administrators and business associates. He knew it was his duty to carry on governing all the possessions his ancestors had accumulated. He affirmed his dedication to continue, even improve, the running of it all. Maturity had caught up with him.

From the free-spirited boy waging local battles of no great significance in Erin, to the administrator of a vast trading empire in western Europe, the transformation was sudden and passionate. Padrig soon grasped that all his official authority and wealth would always come second to the entitled crowned dynasties of the realms where his commerce and land tenures were based; the reality troubled him. Despite being a descendant of a Celtic lineage going back two thousand years, he felt he was considered a lesser class by the heads of states. It was a great shame all the authority and power once bestowed upon his ancestors in Kernow had faded through the ages. His lineage fell to a lesser group, and a clear demarcation had ensued. He came to think all the power he held through financial wealth should be put to work to benefit the Celtic cause as a whole—humiliations and manifest injustice caused by abuse of power by local rulers should be disassembled. There were ways to do so by surreptitious action to diminish and hurt the perpetrators' sovereignty. Padrig thought hard to find a means of harming the established ruling gentry. He had to operate in a stealth-like manner so the consequences would not come back to haunt him, and to avoid reprisals.

In the first instance, Padrig developed a stratagem so the English monarch would take notice. The Crown stored grain and other goods in huge storage areas, mostly around London and in a few other ports. Cereals, oils, wine, and woods were amassed in those facilities. The systematic destruction of the spaces would significantly undermine the House of Plantagenet, and the ingenious circumstance was that he, Padrig, supplied and filled some of those. They were mostly goods bought with the proceeds of levees on the population. He devised an elaborate scheme so it would be practically impossible to trace the clandestine actions back to him. He created a network of hermetic relationships, at various levels, none of whom knew each other. It had to be highly structured, but he thought it worth doing—it would be the map of his destiny.

The first person Padrig approached was Ralloch who had been appointed by Padrig as the keeper of the properties in Telscombe in Sussex. Telscombe which had been bestowed to the Trestan branch had been transferred to the Padrig branch by royal decree which granted the transfer of the deeds. Ralloch's loyalty and devotion for his master was absolute. For reason of trust, the wardens of Telscombe had always been men with a Breton connection since Trestan had been awarded the domain. Ralloch was no exception, he was the descendant of a Breton warrior who had fought at the battle of Senlac. Meeting in Gwened, Padrig told Ralloch of his ideas to rectify the current treatment of the Celts by the Plantagenet administration. Ralloch, in having to endure constant pressure and humiliation by the rulers of England, did not need much prompting to show interest in the venture. Ralloch was to recruit someone to start fires in the royal warehouses. He knew a distant relative who lived in London; a man placed highly in the capital's underworld. The relative, Steffen, specialised in advancing money to wretched people with gambling debt, or were victims of blackmail.

Ralloch and Steffen met in London to devise a plan to burn down one of the grain warehouses upriver from the Tower of London. Ralloch explained it was his idea, motivated by his resentment of the English tax collectors. Although Steffen thought it bizarre, he understood his cousin's impetus and believed the idea emanated from Ralloch alone. Steffen knew a fellow named Gallin who could be persuaded to do such a deed. Gallin was a force of nature but got into debt with gamblers and had upset the wrong crowd. He had come to Steffen before who had obliged, but the leniency was wearing thin. Gallin was at the end of his rope and was grateful of an option bearing possible solution to his self-created tribulations.

On meeting, Steffen told Gallin he wanted the warehouses burned as he had a large load of illicit grain to get rid of and as long as the royal warehouses were full, they were his constant competitor. It made perfect sense to the immoral mind of Gallin.

The enclosure was a square block. Access to the grain storage was via the main entrance on the north side of the river Thames embankment. The gate was monitored by two soldiers and inside, a watchman was on constant duty. Ralloch told Steffen the sentries felt sorry for themselves working a rest day—Sundays—and the watchman was most likely to doze off. A wall, about twenty feet high, surrounded the area storing the grain. The silos had few openings; vertical slide flaps at the bottom, lids at the apex. Wooden steps led to the top where a trap door made it possible to dump the grains into the storage turrets. Ralloch had acquired his information from a grain merchant to whom he sold the Telscombe Manor produce.

The plan was to throw a grapnel over the outer wall of the west side, then use the same rope to go down into the inner yard and climb the ladder of a silo furthest away from the gate. The watchman's space was to the right of the gate therefore to the east, and his vision was cut off from that which lay on the west side. Gallin was to carry three bundles of cord impregnated with a flammable tar, set them alight and throw them into the silo. It would take at least a good five minutes for the flames to catch and about twenty minutes before a raging fire would take over the silo thus leaving plenty of time for Gallin to vanish from the site. The plan had to be executed in the summer, preferably July, as the relative dryness of the atmosphere would make chance of the fire spreading through natural occurrence more plausible. That it would happen on a Sunday was established but it needed to be a night when the moon's light was dim and after midnight when darkness was preponderant. Steffen did not fully trust Gallin so would inconspicuous, observing nearby.

At last, the day of reckoning was upon them. For safety, Padrig did not know the details, nor the day and hours. On the third Sunday of the month of July, Gallin made his approach. Taking the grapnel out of a sack, he whirled it around and hurled it in such a way it shot upwards and got stacked on top. Gallin proceeded to climb by walking upwards on the surface of the wall. The manoeuvre was complicated as Gallin had a sack attached by a string around his waist. After much effort, he reached the top, dropped the rope down the inside of the wall, scaled down twenty feet, then climbed onto the makeshift ladder of a silo nearest to his point of landing. Once on top, Gallin had extreme difficulty opening the turret flaps. He hoped his grunts of exertion would not carry over to the guardhouse—thankfully, they did not. He took out from his sack a charred-cloth and efficiently created a spark from a flint-and-steel apparatus then lit the cord bundles impregnated with flammable tar. The concoction started showing smoke and tiny flames. He tossed everything in the hole but stayed on top to make sure all proceeded as intended. He closed the flaps and went down the precarious ladder. The rope was still hanging down on the inside of the wall. He realised it had been risky to leave it in full view of a sentinel doing his rounds. Fortunately, nobody had come around. Everything was quiet, he made his escape and disappeared into the darkness of the night.

Flames did not come into view from out of the silo until half an hour after ignition. An hour later, an adjacent silo caught fire. Passers-by started to notice the sizeable blaze; the sentries were outside the walls of the enclosure where all the silos were now burning. More soldiers arrived but could do little except watch in disbelief.

The wind was coming from the west, and the fire moved east towards the Tower of London. By the time it abated, the sinister incident had burned about one hundred acres, including adjacent structures.

There were no suspicions at first as people were so preoccupied with the manner in which it spread. Rain and a fading wind had finally stopped it. No one had been seen in the vicinity. The incident, people believed, was caused by the hot weather and it had happened before that a chemical reaction within a silo could self-ignite.

Two months followed, and although the smell of the smouldering ashes still lingered in the air, everyone had discarded thoughts of the huge fire. It would have remained a mystery were it not for Gallin getting drunk in a tavern and shouting at the top of his voice that natural causes did not start the silo fires but rather a human-made deed. Without him noticing, two gentlemen followed him on his way home. They followed him to an agglomeration of buildings in the north of the city. Gallin entered a large portal leading into a quad surrounded by buildings three storeys high and completely enclosing the square. The two followers decided not to go in; they feared they could be seen and questioned.

It so happened, the two gentlemen were part of the royal household and when they heard Gallin mentioning the fire, they immediately thought about the great concern the king's entourage had shown with the loss of such valuable commodity. One of them went to the tower to explain what they had heard, garner some help, and seek direction. The other stayed, readied to stand for a long time and keep an eye on the comings and goings of the building's occupants. Surveying the area, he saw no discernible exit. His partner returned about three in the morning, accompanied by half a dozen armed men. There was no question they would enter the building; it was highly likely, in that part of town, individuals of the underworld resided there. Caution was of the essence. The two men who originally overheard Gallin were tiring quickly but needed to stay awake for identification purposes. They decided one would sleep three hours then take over the next shift. Not until mid-morning was Gallin seen going out through the main portal. By now the pursuers were pretty well organised. Once the initial spotters identified Gallin to a group of four disguised men of arms, they left the scene for a well-earned rest.

Gallin walked as if he did not have a care in the world. He was heading west of the city and finally, when in a tavern, met with a couple of men; the meeting had nothing to do with the fire. Steffen had told Gallin their contact was to cease regardless if the incident was successful or not. Steffen suggested Gallin leave London and get lost in nature. *This* meeting was about planning a robbery in the distant future.

Gallin was prey for his followers, but he did not know it. As long as he was in a crowded environment, his would-be attackers could not get to him. They had to wait until the evening to subdue him in a deserted alley... the opportunity came. They hit him behind the head with the pommel of one of the aggressor's sword. They dragged him for a while as if he had passed out like a drunkard. They finally got into the tower after having hit him repeatedly, so he was unconscious during the journey. They tied him with shackles to a huge table used for interrogation and torture. They let him wake up by himself, and when he did so, he started shouting abuse.

Gallin was not a man to suffer for anybody if he could help it. When he saw a sword being heated so red it was nearly melting, he shouted that he knew who did it. Gallin told them, having been approached by a man named Steffen asking to set fire to the royal grain storage, he had refused but he was sure Steffen would have found somebody else to do it. This was the reason he was not surprised when the news went around London that the silos and adjacent buildings had burned. He told them Steffen was a financier of the underworld and a planner of numerous thefts but he, Gallin, never became involved in the action. When asked where Steffen could be found, Gallin said he was usually in a tavern north of the tower. One of the interrogators had his doubts about Gallin's account, and drawing his knife, he placed it on Gallin's stomach.

'I am about to pierce your organs with this, so tell me the truth, or you will be in Hell within an instant.'

'I admit I was the perpetrator, but Steffen was the mastermind I knew nothing of the motive.'

The interrogators proceeded to put the admitted suspect in a horse and carriage and went towards the said tavern.

They waited a few hours, then an hour before midnight, Steffen was seen entering the drinking hole. When he left a few hours later, he was with another man. Both were subjugated and, like Gallin the night before, taken to the tower where they were left in shackles for two days. In the evening of the second day, the other man was interrogated and released, as he had nothing to do with the silo affair and had convinced them so. He was set free but followed in case he led to others. The king's men were convinced there was an extensive network and it was worthwhile to be patient and catch the "big fish" if there was one. The name of the man they released was Warril; he spoke with a Welsh accent.

Steffen was kept in isolation for another full day. The Norman knights who were to interrogate him wanted to know where he was from, his life history, and his motive for burning the grain storage.

Do I tell them what I know and my connection to Ralloch, or do I endure and act as if I know nothing? Betraying Ralloch would be hard but how much can I endure?'

Steffen had instructed Warril to warn Ralloch, but he had second thoughts; perhaps it was not his best decision, they might have him followed. Although Warril knew nothing of the conspiracy, he would get compromise all the same—Steffen decided to bear torture. It was not long before he was chained to a huge stone table. Questions were asked, answers were not forthcoming. Swords were used to draw lines of blood all over his chest. That was bearable, but the pain and terror intensified as they proceeded to extract one of his toenails. As the third one was being removed, he let them know he was prepared to talk. The sight of his bleeding toes and his lacerated chest nearly made him faint.

Steffen told them everything.

'Ralloch is my cousin and he approached me; I subsequently recruited Gallin. Ralloch is the warden of a manor in Sussex but I do not know precisely where. Ralloch wanted to get back at the tax collectors and royal authorities as he felt they had unfairly treated him. Being cousins, I felt obliged to help. My ancestors came from Brittany a long time ago and fought with the Normans at the Battle of Hastings.' This was untrue.

The interrogation stopped; they had no need to kill him now but would keep him imprisoned. They would research the records to find the actual owner of a manor in Sussex who could have ties with Brittany. *Why a Breton?* There was high probability this ethnic group only trusted people of the same blood. It was pointless to try and catch Ralloch, he could be anywhere. Warril was being followed, that would bring outcome enough.

Going through Royal records, they discovered Telscombe Manor had been granted to a Breton noble after the Battle of Hastings and handed down to another Breton called Padrig.

Chapter Twenty-Six

While all these events were taking place on Big Island, Padrig was in Breizh in his Gwened domain. The royal investigators were confident Ralloch was implicated, but they had no proof Padrig was part of the scheme. Padrig had no inkling of what happened after the burning of the silos. As far as he was concerned, everything went as planned and the royal authorities had no lead as to the perpetrators.

For the Plantagenet agents, Warril was a thread to lead them to Ralloch; the other path lay to Telscombe Manor. The men at arms went, and to their delight, Ralloch was there. He had not heard about the arrests and had no idea he was suspected of being the mastermind behind the scheme. Great was his dismay when twenty soldiers ransacked the manor, seizing documents and objects.

Ralloch was put in chains and transported on horseback to the castle of Lewes where his captors tortured him in an especially violent manner—nail extraction, deep sword cuts, beaten so hard both his forearms were broken. They punched his face so much, he could not see through his swollen eyelids. By the fourth day, he was in such a permanent daze he no longer knew if he was dead or alive. He thought he was floating and seeing his wounded body beneath him. The pain had caused such an unreal feeling, he just wanted to die and be delivered of all his agonies, but his torturers would relent in their deeds and the will to stay alive would return. Ralloch felt his infliction so great, he would never recover. The repeated torture sessions blurred his mind, nevertheless he had moments of clarity; he knew his fate was sealed and they would execute him regardless. Therefore, he embarked on a series of lies which told them succinctly the conspiracy came from abroad, but was orchestrated by the King of France who felt continually oppressed by the English power on French territory. Known for his bitterness towards the Plantagenet, agents of the French king had approached Ralloch. He conveyed his contacts had long gone, back across the Channel—he invented names.

The torture stopped and the royal investigators turned their attention to the French colony in London. Ralloch now just had to wait for his death, which he hoped would be by hanging or beheading so it would not be so unbearable. He has guessed correctly; his sentence was death. Moreover, the execution had to take place in France, in the town of Tours, within the Plantagenet realm.

Padrig heard Ralloch would be put to death publicly and decided to go undercover with bodyguards. He felt it a gesture he owed Ralloch.

The day arrived and the large square in front of the cathedral was where the death sentence, by dismemberment, would be carried out. Mid-morning, the wounded body of Ralloch was tied by his arms above his head, and by his feet. The ropes were linked to two wrenches, one on each side of the table where he lay. His cries of agony lasted for thirty minutes before he passed away. His corpse was beheaded, and his head paraded for all to see.

Padrig stayed for a while and tried to show no emotion. He suspected many of the King of England's agents were in the crowd looking for clues to lead them to accomplices not yet uncovered. He and his bodyguards moved away and made the journey back to Gwened. Padrig knew it would be impossible for him to go back to England as sooner or later he would be found out. Even Brittany was becoming a dangerous location; he would be traced there as well. Eire and Scotland seemed to be the only hiding places where he could circulate in relative tranquillity. In doing so, he would forsake a significant part of his assets.

Without notice, Padrig sailed on one of his ships from Gwened through the Morbihan Gulf and made for the harbour of Oban where he tried to pick up the pieces of his mercantile empire. He reflected whether or not it had been worth it to try and take on the Plantagenet—it certainly looked like he had lost. However, he was welcoming a simplification of his life. The long bloodline that had started in the ancestral land more than twenty centuries ago was yet again changing path and this time going north to Celtic Scotland. Padrig, with his Irish and Breton blood, would not be mistaken for a native, but his notoriety as a trader and merchant ensured many doors would open for him. His fortune, even slashed in half, was still significant although he was not as land rich as he used to be.

Padrig found quite a few of the local gentry sympathetic to his fate; they did not particularly care for the rulers of England. Scotland had just freed itself from a brief period of judication from the Henry II Plantagenet tutelage.

The Breton busied his time maintaining his commerce between Scotland and Eire. Often, he sailed to his suppliers in Southern Europe; he had to rebuild every link and recreate new ways to trade. His bond with Brittany was only kept alive by visits from old partners or friends who had not forgotten he had once de facto been the most powerful individual in Breizh.

The line of Padrig and his ancestors were back on Big Island after seven centuries. He missed Breizh's rugged coastline and the wilderness of its interior. Brittany was inexorably heading towards losing its individuality; the rulers were leaning towards a rapprochement with the French kingdom, and every marriage was causing the dilution of the Breton ruling classes away from their Celtic character.

The *Breton war of succession* was between two families who were more French than Breton, and one of them had leaned toward the English. The Hundred Years War (1337–1453) saw Brittany hover more toward England than France. The *coup de grâce* came when Anne de Bretagne, marrying her second King of France, offered her country to the French kingdom. That was the final draw to regularise a slow but deliberate move toward full annexation. Brittany still had a parliament, and of all the French provinces, it was the one with the most independence. The people, however, had stayed Breton, Celt, and for them to be French did not signify their belonging to a bigger kingdom. The tempering in the Celtic blood of the ruling classes was not crucial for the ordinary folks of Brittany. As time went on, France was getting more and more involved in the affairs of the Duchy and consequences were for everybody to notice.

The more prominent non-Celtic kingdoms were putting pressure on the Celts. In Scotland, it resulted in the massacre of Glencoe and Culloden; Scots betrayed Scots to win the favour of England. In Ireland, the implantation of English lords gave an excuse for Cromwell to invade. How they got the land in the first place was the result of compromises, with the premise if they gave a little, they would not lose everything. The future was to prove this a tragic mistake. Wales was moderately infiltrated, yet the local gentry had to survive and yielded their sovereignty. The same took place in Cornwall, and they lost their freedom in a tacit arrangement with the British Crown.

Padrig's descendants resided mainly in the west of Scotland. The link with Brittany and the distant legacy of Ervar was not wholly forgotten even if it was twenty-five centuries old.

Chapter Twenty-Seven

Five centuries had gone by and a descendant of Padrig was the Earl of Ardbein. The earl was a laird in the west of Scotland and a high-ranking officer in a Highland regiment. He was taking part in the landing at Quiberon with the British navy helping French Royalists form a front to combat the Republicans. It was the middle of the French revolution in the 1790's. Ardbein had a special mission to complete—he was to get "lost", contact the leaders of covert fighters dedicated to the French Monarchist cause, find out how they operated, what their strengths and weaknesses were, and what they needed. The information gathered was to be transmitted back to British Intelligence by the earl when he went back to London. Ardbein hardly spoke French and even less Breton. Somehow, he managed to escape the debacle of the landing, and he disappeared in the countryside. He knew the principal leaders of the rebellion were in hiding in the region of Treveleg, now renamed Plumelec. He also knew roughly seven hundred years ago his ancestors lived in the area and were landed nobility. To get into the vicinity of

Plumelec was no simple task. Ardbein only had an imprecise map of the region, barely legible due to spots of salty water caused by walking in the sea to get to the beach. He was dressed in what English Intelligence and French Émigrés thought a Breton peasant would wear; actually, looking like a Breton peasant could be dangerous as the Republicans troops viewed the locals as rebels.

Eventually Ardbein arrived where he was presumed to meet relevant contacts who worked with George Cadoudal, the indestructible chief of the Breton insurgence. Ardbein's goal and Cadoudal's objective were entirely different. Cadoudal wanted the French royalty reinstated and a semi-autonomous Brittany. Ardbein's continuing mission was to start investigating the possibility of a Breton independence, completely separated from France and restoring the old Duchy, which would be an ally of Britain on the continent, and fight the common enemy, the French Republic. He was led to a hamlet on top of a wooded hill called Kerihuel. There in the main room of a farm, with a big chimney fire, and around a rectangular table, sat three men dressed like peasants. One of them had bushy hair and a face a size above average; it was George Cadoudal.

Cadoudal, expressed himself in perfect English. 'Welcome to our part of the world. I am glad to see you survived the journey. Are you hungry?'

'I am glad finally to be where my mission takes me. No thank you. I am too exhausted to eat anything right now.'

'Unfortunately we cannot offer you repose here; we never know when we will have to move. It could be in five minutes or three hours. Vigilance is our friend. The locals are friendly to our cause but once they have alcohol in their bodies, one can never tell with whom they will confer the little they know about us. Therefore, I will tell you what is in store for you during your stay in Brittany. You will be taken to three places where we have significant troops. That way you will be able to judge our strengths and our shortcomings. You will travel at night with my trusted Mathurin Le Breton as a guide.'

'When do we start marching?'

'At two o'clock in the morning; first stop is a camp in the Brocéliande forest. Even if you are not from around here, you must have heard the name of the large wood made famous by the Arthurian Legend.'

Ardbein wanted to say he was well versed in the history and his roots were deeper on that land than Cadoudal's but it was not the right moment.

At two, Ardbein started his long trek with Mathurin. They never walked in the middle of the roads and paths, instead they stuck to the sides. When day broke, they moved onto the other side of the hedges and walked in the fields. When human activities occurred, they crouched on the ground against the hedges.

They finally arrived in Brocéliande and from nowhere, Chouans appeared. The word Chouan came from the French *chouette*, meaning owl. They used howling as a way of communicating in the dark, hence the name. The visitors were escorted to one of the rebel chiefs who went by the *nom de guerre*, Josselin Trentin. Ardbein handed him the letter Cadoudal had written. It stated the envoy from the British was to be shown training exercises, arms handling... in other words, anything, which would show him the professionalism of the Royalist Army.

Ardbein was most impressed by the manner in which everyman could camouflage himself at a moment's notice. It was unpredictable how that stealth legion kept emerging and vanishing; it was actually scary, and Ardbein wondered if he was dealing with ghosts. He spent two full days with the army—the fierceness and physical ability of the rebels was impressive especially as their weaponry was disparate, and they lacked small canons. Foot hauling provided the mobility; it had the advantage to traverse any kind of terrain despite the hampered firepower. The nocturnal activities were primordial, and Ardbein wondered when they got respite. (The other two locations showed the same proficiency in undercover warfare.)

At the final meeting, Ardbein candidly told the chief rebel he was impressed by the quality of his troops and their method of fighting; he would recommend sending more arms. George Cadoudal acquiesced what was said but did not think for a moment anything would come of it. The war was an affair between Bretons and French, between Royalists and Republicans. He did not trust the English to do anything, believing they had ulterior motives. That Ardbein might have ancient roots in the local land... that was probably true, but that was so many years ago that he probably viewed the world as an Englishman, not a Breton.

Ardbein was back in London within a week through arranged passage in a small vessel that he boarded in the Gulf of Morbihan. He met straight away with an intelligence officer from the Admiralty where all his observations were duly recorded. He was not sure if they would involve him in the follow-up and if any decisive actions would be taken.

A few weeks went by, and Ardbein was asked to present himself at the Admiralty headquarters in London. He did not know what to expect but was excited at the prospect of learning something new.

It turned out the meeting was one-sided in the sense the ministry man in charge of the project, wearing civilian clothes and a wig, was doing all the talking, even answering his own questions. Ardbein realised the man had no regard for the Bretons and Brittany, for him they were all French and he had chosen to ignore the subtlety of the ethnic difference.

The Scot became increasingly upset listening to this arrogant civil servant. He felt the English were mixing up a lot of issues. Not seeing the distinction between Bretons and French was the same as not understanding disparity concerning Scots and English. The government of His Majesty George III was only interested in using the excuse of "helping" the Chouan army so they could be a barnacle in the rear of the French Republicans. They greatly misunderstood the feelings of the Bretons towards the United Kingdom. Brittany and England might have been allied four centuries ago during the Hundred Years War, however when it came to maritime matters, they had been fighting for an eon. Jacques Cartier, the founder of French Canada, was from St Malo, as was Surcouf, a Breton privateer who never missed an opportunity to pound on any British vessel he could find. They both saw the English as enemies whenever they met on the open seas.

Ardbein was ordered back to Brittany, not only to supervise the supplies for the rebels but also to ferret out the leaders who would collaborate with the British. Ardbein took a few deep breaths before he could fathom the implications of carrying on the mission. It was a duty he had to perform but he did not really believe the merit of the orders. For the government, it was just an alley to explore; if there were any positive results, it would help in the destruction of the French Republic and keep a foothold in that part of France.

A few weeks later, back in Brittany, Ardbein met clandestinely in the forest of Brocéliande with one of Cadoudal's lieutenants. He felt a tightness in his stomach when he told the Breton the government of his gracious majesty would deliver more fighting supplies if, in return, they would prepare the way for a bridgehead of twenty thousand British troops to defend and administer the province. If the British were to commit so many soldiers and so much money, they had to make sure the running of the region would not hinder their objective.

After delivering his ultimatum of sorts, Ardbein felt like he had spewed a spoiled piece of food and was relieved. He had no doubt in his mind his message would produce some interesting reactions from the Chouans.

The response came under the form of a demand from George Cadoudal himself. Ardbein was led, blindfolded, to a house; he guessed it was near Plumelec but could not be sure.

Cadoudal met his guest in the eye and spoke, his deep cavernous voice commanding the situation.

'Monsieur Ardbein, you can transmit to your superiors that in no circumstances will the Royalist rebellion, and what we are fighting for, serve the interest of his Britannic Majesty. The thought of being subjugated to the English and becoming their puppets is quite horrendous to me. Our fight against the French Republic is between them and us. Help with such conditions, which the British would impose no doubt, would enslave us to the manoeuvring of your government. With the French, we know what to expect, and our differences are plenty, but at least they are direct. Good day sir.'

Ardbein had never been so humiliated, but deep down, he was glad the Chouans had reacted in that fashion.

Before returning to England, Ardbein wanted to go back to Plumelec and find some of the descendants of his ancestors. The main branch was called Le Breton, the reason being, the area had for centuries adopted the French language although Breton was still spoken as well as a mix of the two languages called Gallo. Gallo had no rules and varied from village to village. The ancient Celts who were there before AD 500 were the majority in Plumelec, then called Treveleg. The newcomers from Britain were judged the outsiders, and to emphasise the point, they were named Le Breton, identifying them as being the direct descendants of the latter settlers from Big Isle.

Enquiring around, Ardbein found a Le Breton family who was possibly related to him through several generations. He befriended them and became close to the eldest daughter, Terrick. When he was ready to leave for Britain, he was granted her parents' permission to take her with him. Terrick was of fair complexion, blue eyes, and dark hair. She stood very straight—as she was quite short, she did not want to lose any height. She was by all accounts a beauty, at least Ardbein thought so. Her temperament was vivacious, and she had a fast tongue that could shut off anybody at a moment's notice. The two of them rode to the north coast of Brittany where a sloop took them to Southampton, then on to London.

Ardbein decided on the return journey to leave his job; he hoped his commanders would let him go without a fuss. He explained the latest standpoint from the Chouan point of view to his superiors. Soon after, he tendered his resignation and travelled by Mail Post carriages to Glasgow and the west of Scotland to his estate near Glencoe and Fort William.

The irony of history made it so when Cadoudal felt his insurgency faltering, he sought refuge in England and became the pathetic plotter and puppet of the English to assassinate Napoleon. He was caught and executed in France. He was unrepentant to the end against the republican ideas, and always loyal as to the integrity of Brittany.

Ardbein's latest assignment left him with considerable doubt and questioning his intellectual honesty in doing something he thought wrong. The Bretons were pawns in British policy; the independence "carrot" put in front of their noses was not real. His Majesty's government held little feeling for the Celts across the sea; no more than those Celts in the United Kingdom.

Ardbein could have kept busy just looking after his estate and the remnants of the trading company started by distant ancestors. However, everywhere he looked, he saw oppressed Celtic people, from Ireland to Brittany, and right on his doorstep, the clearing of the highlands. A lot of them hired their services to armies governed by countries acting as tyrants over their own people.

The clearance of the Scottish Highlands was still in everyone's memory north of Glasgow and Edinburgh; the humiliation and viciousness of the repression after Culloden were uncalled for; the English went beyond the limit of pure cruelty. The paradox being, within the border regions, the Celts in Devon, Cornwall, Cumbria, and Wales were being assimilated. They became servile or wanted to fit in and distanced themselves from their genetic identity. In Ireland, parts of Scotland, and Brittany, their unique character persisted.

The Nineteenth Century saw repression by the colonising forces. Before the British went to Africa and the rest of the world, it was essential, inside their own country, for everything to be subjugated. That very action fomented reactions which caused the resurgence of Celtic nationalism. Ireland led the way and was to pay dearly for it.

Celtic identity was revived in Wales and Brittany by way of cultural efforts via literature.

Ardbein and Terrick had a son, Fulgor, who carried on the business traditions of his ancestors. Celtic brotherhood and a sense of belonging to that race were indifferent to him. He revived the trading company and travelled extensively throughout Europe and the Americas; he exported and imported goods from region to region. He spoke English, Gaelic, Breton, French, Spanish, and German. Fulgor married a Scottish lady called Wilma and they had one daughter whom they named Emma. She in turn had a long courtship and eventually married the son of an associate of her father, a Welsh fellow called Gareth who helped in the dynasty mercantile trade. Of this union, a son, Gildas, was born, named in remembrance of the founder saint of Brittany.

Gildas was interested in religion and studied theology at Queen's College, Oxford. When his father was getting old, Gildas went back to Scotland and became acquainted with the family firm which had established headquarters in Edinburgh. It was late in life for him, but Gildas threw himself, body and soul, into the endeavour. He married Mary, a much younger woman, from Baltimore, America.

The company had been named Ardbein Breton Company, known as ABC over the world, at least in the western realms. Gildas and Mary had a new-born, Arvor, in 1895.

Arvor received his education at Edinburgh University and was only mildly interested in involving himself with the family's trading affairs. Once all the elders had died, he placed several trusted men in charge of managing the business. He left Edinburgh and moved to Fort William. The Western Highlands had been the region where his great-grandfather had lived, and he was well aware of the history of his ancestors.

Chapter Twenty-Eight

County Tipperary, Ireland in the 1920's; Arvor's palms were sweaty, his forehead dripped with perspiration, his hands trembled, his vision was blurred. He was taking part in an ambush against British soldiers. He could hear the noise of a convoy of lorries getting nearer. His instructions were to shoot and empty his magazine when the convoy was halfway passed him. He was hidden among a thicket, looking north. Between him and the road, there was a slope, and on the other side there were the rest of Irish fighters. He had no doubt in his mind he would squeeze the trigger; being judged by his superiors was more frightening than getting shot by the British soldiers.

When the convoy passed at half of its own length, Arvor fired, aiming at the driver of one of the vehicles. All the lorries stopped, and soldiers leapt off them. As they started scaling up towards the sniper, they came under heavy fire from across the road, the volleys were sustained by at least a dozen shooters. The Brits were getting shot in the back, and as they turned around one hundred and eighty degrees, they became targets from both sides.

The shots vanished as quickly as they had been initiated. Arvor pulled the first trigger; he was not a Catholic, he was not Irish, he was a Scot from the western isles and spoke Gaelic which made it convenient for him to converse with the Irish. The two languages had the same roots and therefore similarities. His Celtic identity had been oppressed, and as there was, so far, no significant Celtic revival movement in Scotland, he espoused the Irish Nationalist cause.

Miles away, around the same time, toward the south-east in Brittany, a small group of young students, under cover of night, were busy placing plastic charges under the statue of Anne de Bretagne, in their opinion, the whore who married the king of France and changed forever an already declining Breton realm.

The clock was set for four in the morning, and when the explosion went off, window glasses broke and a whole district awoke, but the statue was crippled beyond recognition. The symbolic action had not been lost on those who knew their history... Breton history.

In the western world, Celtic people, to the observer, had reached the bottom of the wave. An uncoordinated revival was on its way; it had no plans and was not orchestrated by any grassroots movement. The humiliations endured by the downtrodden people; they had reached such a point there *had* to be a reaction.

In North America, the various Celtic groups lived independently, even within the same state, they lived apart with no organisation, they simply tried to survive on a day-to-day basis. Some became so loyal to their new home state, it had the unfortunate consequences of Celts fighting against Celts in wars. The American Civil War was an example of such a disastrous occurrence.

In many countries, such as England and Ireland, very often, the lower strata of society filled the criminal ranks; hence the reason Australia is full of the Irish convicts' descendants. The irony is the penal settlement, instead of being a bastion of Protestantism, became one of Catholicism. Immigration was the answer—the Irish to America and Australia, the Scots to Canada and New Zealand, the Welsh to America and England, the Bretons to Paris, France.

Arvor participated in many skirmishes and lived clandestinely. Through betrayals, he was sought by the occupying authorities. He hid, first in Dublin, then made his way back to Scotland and settled in Glasgow. He took an assumed name and became a joiner for the shipbuilding industry. He could not go back to his estate because it was the first place the British secret service would look. Before joining the Irish cause, he had left a network of intendants to look after his holdings. He had a sophisticated procedure to check what was happening without being traceable.

Shipbuilding joinery was hard work, but there was an element of pride in seeing the final product, a ship. Arvor joined a union; it kept the employer from making mischief at the workers' expense. Most of the workers lived from one pay day to the next, but they felt pride no money could buy—they believed in salvation, hope, and solidarity, apart from feeling free, it gave meanings to their lives. Theirs was a beautiful simplicity; they fed their families, built ships, and belonged to a group which they could not let down nor would it let you down. In several ways, it was like being back in the Celtic tribe of many centuries ago when the core of life was the clan—all were expected to contribute, in return, solidarity and understanding from fellow tribesmen. Many of the shipbuilders were of Irish descent.

Arvor made up his mind to go to America and start a new life in New York City. To leave from a British port might be too dangerous as he did not know if some of his ex-companions in arms from the Irish nationalists might have given his name to the authorities. So, he decided to go to Edinburgh, hang around a Scandinavian freighter, seek work and jump ship once he reached a neutral port. It so happened he boarded a Norwegian vessel and arrived in Bergen.

A few weeks later, a freighter landed Arvor in New York where he went through the inquisitive US Customs. He found himself on the streets of New York, dazzled and somewhat lost. He had been given a contact name at the Caledonian Club, a refuge for Scots in New York, and he hoped they would give him addresses for lodgings, jobs and anything else useful to a newly landed immigrant. The club was run by some old ladies who were kind but of little help. Nevertheless, he secured temporary shelter and some basic food, and for that he was grateful. Arvor only could listen to the other lodgers for hints on where to acquire employment.

Some days after landing, Arvor was in downtown Manhattan on his way to an interview after a tip from one of the Scots. By chance, he fell upon an Irish fellow he had fought with in Ireland, his name was Eamon. They arranged to meet in a pub after the interview, which did not bear any results.

Arvor and Eamon talked for hours about their fighting days, how they got to America, and the present. It turned out Eamon was deeply involved with the Irish community. The Irish in New York, at that time, held many manual labour jobs, and were at an advantage over other ethnic groups, they spoke English and had the support of the influential Catholic Church. Employers always tried to pay them below standard rate and were dishonest as a rule. Eamon explained he belonged to an association of Irish people whose goal was to protect their own, and make employers respect the Irish workforce.

Small acts of sabotage were conducted which impaired the good functioning of the businesses which were not respectful and exploited the sons and daughters of Erin. Eamon told Arvor he would speak about him to his superiors in the organisation. He made Arvor swear whatever the outcome of their conversation, it never took place. The Scot was not surprised, it had been the same law of silence when he was with the Irish rebels back in the island. Transgressing it was a death sentence.

Arvor thought long and hard; he did not come to America to get involved in Irish oppression. On the other hand, the thoughts of the subjugated Celt made him re-kindle the flame of injustice. He also considered how long it would take him to find a job and live decently. Therefore after a few days, he decided to join Eamon's mob, and if they got back to him, he would go ahead. He realised changing his mind was not an option and he would have to endure the third degree from the local chief acting as defender of the children of Erin.

The meeting took place in a cellar in Lower Manhattan. There were three men, four with Eamon. They all wore a tweed jacket and a cap worn with the visor in front, partially covering the eyes because it formed a shadow. Arvor was questioned to find out how dedicated he was to the cause, and how prepared he was to force respect for the Irish, even if it meant doing unlawful actions. Arvor enquired about the nature of the operations they undertook. That raised some eyebrows, but they had been briefed Arvor had killed a few Englishmen in several engagements, so they let it slide. They did not answer directly, but made it understood they could encompass unusual methods. Arvor understood and did not inquire further. After several hours he was dismissed and told they would contact him with their decision.

Arvor returned that evening to the Caledonian Club, took his meal by himself and went to his measly room. He was not sure if he was embarking on a dangerous existence. However, the sense of duty to his breed justified in his mind the decision to become active in whatever was necessary to garner recognition and respect for the Celtic race.

The news of Arvor's admission into the secret vigilant society came. *Was it a guild? A union? A league?* His contact was a man called Tierney, a naturally assumed name, he would be the one to advise instruction. When Tierney needed to get in touch with Arvor, he would leave a sign written in chalk on the cement steps outside the Caledonian Club. If the sign was two slashes Arvor was to turn left, then take the first right street and walk until he could see a bar; it did not have to Irish. Tierney would wait outside, his face partially covered by a scarf. If the sign was a circle, Arvor would turn right, take the first street on the left and walk to the nearest church, Protestant or Catholic, and Tierney would be sitting in the back row on the left of the aisle.

Three weeks after Arvor's admission to the cause, the "two slashes" sign appeared. He turned left, then right and two hundred and fifty yards on the east side of the street, there was a bar, Tierney was inside. Arvor's first assignment was to slash the vehicle tyres of the owner of a construction company in the Bronx. The owner was a German by the name of Horst Birkmester; he was himself somewhat of a recent immigrant and, as was often the case, his motivation to get rich and up the ladder of American society, meant he cut corners, used cheap labour, and took care of the local officials to peddle influence and reap protection. Horst had bilked one Irishman too many, and the "organisation" had decided his rocketing wealth should go sideways for a while. They did not want to cripple his firm, just cause enough damage to force him into decency, and make less profit by paying his workers a living wage.

Birkmester's car was inside the courtyard of his firm. It was easy for Arvor; dressed as a labourer, he slashed the tyres so effectively, the German had to walk home that evening. It was a painful stroll as three huge masked fellows beat him up so well, he had one broken tibia, and a face worked over so harshly he looked like a fleshy mass with no eyes as they were fast shut by the swelling. Both of his hands had been stepped on so hard every bone was broken. Then he was told by a voice, lacking an Irish brogue, to be compassionate towards his workers, and if he were not, he would go to Hell. It seemed bizarre at first, but it left Birkmester thinking the Church, his Church, the Catholic Church was judging him. It left him believing the wrath of God was upon him.

The German's thrashing was only the beginning. Arvor became involved in many such actions. After a while, he convinced himself he was performing a commendable service. The law and order official forces were not on the side of the working folk, so actually, he and his cohorts were on the right side of morality. His superiors were pleased with him and gave him their trust, which was of a paramount factor. Sooner or later, matters were to get pretty serious.

Arvor was summoned to an important meeting in a secret location. He had to go to the Bronx, then Queens where a car was waiting for him. He was blindfolded, which made him nervous; he knew from hearsay, the IRA adopted the same approach to lead a victim to his execution. He estimated he was driven for at least thirty minutes. When the car finally stopped, the blindfold was removed, and he was put in a dark room on a chair facing five masked individuals.

The five men had strong Irish accents and definitely not from Ulster. They had noticed the efficient work Arvor had done, this was their reason for wanting to discuss a project with him. They emphasised if he was ready to hear, he had to swear not to reveal a word, on pain of death. Arvor thought he might be asked to commit murder; he had killed in Ireland during hit and run skirmishes but not in cold blood.

He quickly gathered his thoughts. 'This project... will it serve the Irish people in the US or Ireland, and advance the cause of Celtic people?'

The man seated on the left of the table responded. His deep voice resonated with an impressive yet sinister seriousness.

'You have shown you are concerned by the fate of Irish people who are of course Celtic, but other Celtic nations have not cared much about our fate; the Scots and Welsh-provide soldiers for the British Crown. There is a revival of the Celtic spirit in some parts, but we Irish are basically on our own. You are a Scot by birth, and your defence of the Celts has made you fight our cause in Erin. We, the Irish, are the torchbearers of the Celtic world. We want to be convinced that although you are not Irish, you are true to our ideal because our fight is also the fight of your bloodline. I say this... if you are true to your genes, you ought to be loyal to us.'

'I understand, my soul is deeply immersed in the fate of all Celts oppressed around the world, and the Irish uprising is the only movement acting realistically to further the welfare of our people. So, yes, I am ready to hear what you have to say and keep it secret in my heart.'

'A certain amount of assistance is going back to Ireland to finance the continuous fight against the British. We arrange shipments of weapons but the purchase of those has to be organised outside this country and Ireland itself. Bank robbery has been used in the UK to support clandestine activities. Here, we haven't done anything of the sort. Contributions from the Irish contingent in the United States are not significant because most of the donors are poor. We have decided to rob banks in the New York and Boston area. The Bostonians will rob in New York, and the New Yorkers will do the same in Boston. This is appropriate for security reasons. Therefore, we want you to plan a few raids in Boston. Your education and military training, and having operated under fire, make you a prime candidate to engineer details ensuring the operations run smoothly.'

'Let me express my astonishment and also my gratitude to have the honour of being entrusted with such crucial tasks. Will I be asked to participate physically in such raids?'

'No, you are a planner, not a perpetrator. You will, of course, communicate and plan with the executors.'

Arvor moved to the Boston area. He had "carte blanche" and decided to rent a dwelling in Gloucester, the fishing harbour, north of the city on the coast. He reasoned there were probably too many law enforcement agencies monitoring Irish activities in Boston itself.

Arvor got on to his job, identifying prospects for robbery on institutions which carried a lot of cash. However, banks were frequent targets, with the prohibition and the rising of gangs, there was increased surveillance; besides there was too much competition. He decided to broaden his outlook—the booty from future robberies was to be jewels and gold. For that purpose, he started studying the jewel wholesale market of Rhode Island state. Historically, Providence was the main jewel-making centre. It was an activity which started in the

Eighteenth Century. Most of the raw material was gold, and it chiefly came by train from the Abitibi greenstone belt of Ontario. Therefore, he decided to have a look at the railway depot in Providence. There were no fences, and it was easy to access. For several days, Arvor watched the unloading of goods. The gold, which was already in bullion, was apparently impossible to detect but astute observation of the way the porters handled the shipment made it evident to him what it was.

Arvor rented a motorcycle under a false name and started to follow the tracks. They invariably ended up in Henderson Street where most of the jewellery manufacturers were. His next task was to find a way to ambush the trucks between the railway depot and Henderson Street. It also had to be near the water, on the river where a small rapid boat could wait ready to go to the high sea and make contact with a trawler.

The plan was taking shape. From the railway depot, the van transporting the bullion would take Charter Street then Canal Street. When the vehicle went over the bridge on Providence River, linking Angell Street to the east and Exchange Terrace to the west, it was to be stopped, attacked and emptied of the bullion by hand. The gold would be thrown on a small boat which would head down the Seekonk River and the high seas where a fishing boat with no identification would go towards Nova Scotia.

The scheme had to be presented and approved by the hierarchy in New York City. Arvor was sure the plan was a good one but was worried he would have to settle for men New York would send him. He did not know many people in the organisation, and he had no means of choosing the right ones.

Arvor went to New York and sat for two full days with the movement's strategists. They were impressed by the plan, and there was serious discussion on how to make it work. The prize was high but the execution minutia complicated. They told Arvor to come back in two weeks, and they would work on the personnel necessary to accomplish the holdup.

When the fortnight was over, the go-ahead was granted, and the details extensively reviewed. Arvor was master of the operation in Providence but would not take a direct part in the holdup. Instead, his presence was required in the area where the bullion would be dropped in the boat. Arvor had to coordinate with the captain for the transfer time of the bullion arriving from the coast. The heads in New York managed to charter a high sea fishing boat from Irish fishermen based in Fall River. They were assured the crew was dedicated to help *"Free Ireland"* and sworn to secrecy.

The day of the hijacking finally arrived. The van transporting the bullion was stopped over the bridge, and the occupants beaten, gagged and tied up. Four armed men dressed in railwaymen uniforms kept the scene free of interference, stopping onlookers from getting too close. They all wore masks and refrained from talking. The speedboat, layered with cushions, stood as it took its new cargo. Finally, a rope ladder was thrown over the bridge, and all the participants scaled down into the boat. One man stayed, picked up the road ladder and went into a stolen car with fake number plates. The rope would not be traced forensically, no shots were fired, and no trace of the theft remained. The uniforms were discarded once on board. Eyewitnesses saw the boat and could give a description, but that was all. Arvor stood at a vantage point and saw the operation was conducted without incident. He went back to New York by car that very day. The speed boat was sunk once it delivered its cargo of bullion and men.

Arvor resumed his normal life, which was uneventful. However, he did venture to enquire how the golden cargo had fared. His superiors told him it was a successful operation and had helped the cause. They did not provide any more details.

During this period, the fight for complete independence of the Emerald Isle was on. The six counties to the north were still administrated by the British Crown, and the Catholics were denied jobs and voting rights. The struggle would go on for many decades with hate, terror and many deaths to stand account.

Chapter Twenty-Nine

Arvor resumed his life in New York and waited to hear from the management team of the Irish organisation. He started being troubled by the lifestyle. The fights in the Irish revolt in Ireland, heading delicate operations, and the entire involvement felt hollow after a while. It was time for him to reassess his goal in life. He was, after all, from Scottish gentry with Breton ancestry, and the wealth he could not touch.

Arvor decided, after a few months of idleness, he had to move on. Furthermore, he never heard from the New York Irish top brass; he thought it strange considering the success of the Providence operation. He had to let them know he wanted to go back to Europe—they would probably take his news unfavourably. It crossed his mind they would not let him go as he knew too much and they would eliminate him. It had happened time and again with that sort of secret organisation. They operated under their own rules, which had nothing to do with standard legal systems. He decided to leave without informing anyone of his intentions, however, there were some logistical problems to overcome.

Arvor still had some money under the names of corporations he owned in Scotland, Switzerland and France. He had cash reserves on the continent, but in Scotland and the rest of the United Kingdom, his worth was mostly in property; a company based in Norway ran the administration. The lawyer running it only knew a man from a Swiss bank in Lausanne. Arvor checked in with the Helvetic contact regularly.

A month later, Arvor landed in Genoa and made his way to Lausanne on Lake Leman. He had decided to move to Brittany, land of his distant ancestors. Living in the British Isles was out of the question.

During his visit to Switzerland, Arvor elected to sell all his property in the United Kingdom. He went to Oslo to confer with the Norwegian administrator who would handle the sale; the proceeds would be channelled to Sweden. After having taken care of his administrative duties, Arvor headed for Cherbourg. He sought an isolated location; the islands of Brehat off the northern coast of Brittany.

It was the middle of winter, and he had no problem finding a small farmhouse. His French was reasonably fluent with an Anglo-Saxon accent.

Lying low for a few weeks, Arvor took long walks on those wild and contained islands linked by a short and narrow bridge. He took his meals in the same restaurant and as he was quiet and reserved, the owner refrained from asking him anything. He visited the church on South Island as he wanted to contact the priest.

The name of the cleric was Erwann Gwendal; he spoke Breton and was a fervent activist of keeping Breton particularism in the whole of Brittany. Very often the ministers were the guardians of Breton identity. It was a remnant of the fact the French Revolution a century and a half earlier had taken what little independence the old Duchy had under the French royalty. The persecution of Catholic priests had not been forgotten. Several of them were outright nationalists and wanted a separate country away from France. The rural clergy in small villages, with their allied women inhabitants, were undeniably the rulers. The plague of alcoholism, common to Celtic nations, was rampant. Many men were away for a long time if fishermen, in the naval forces or the merchant navy. The sea was their livelihood and too often a widow maker.

Arvor's conversation with the priest was illuminating. Father Gwendal was interested that Arvor had lived in Ireland, Scotland and the United States. Arvor kept quiet about his deep involvement fighting for the Celtic causes. He listened intensely to the priest who told him an entirely different history of Brittany, not known universally. It was an opener into the ever-persistent hearty Breton soul which had never died since they left Big Island, Britain. It was a history of constant stubbornness in a fight to the death against extinction. Language, music, history could not die, and that was the reason the priest preached from the pulpit in Breton.

A month later, Father Gwendal took Arvor by car to the inner part of the country, about seventy kilometres due south. They crossed the narrow channel to the mainland in a little rowing boat owned by the clergyman and named

"Ma doué"; an expression used a lot in Brittany, a mix of French and Breton, meaning "My God". The inner part of the countryside was densely forested, and the narrow road followed streams for the most part. They finally reached their destination, a small farm at the end of a mud path. As soon as they stopped the car, a man came out of the door. His appearance was striking; he had long grey hair, an aquiline nose, and dark sunken eyes. He wore a black velvet sleeveless vest, a white shirt, and brownish corduroy trousers. Clogs were on his bare feet, and straw was seen protruding from his footwear.

All quickly went inside. It was a typical old Breton house—a single room with areas allocated to different functions such as cooking, eating and sleeping. They sat at the big table where the conversation quickly turned to Celtic identity, culture, history, and shared values.

Arvor felt at home, here was a man who had the same state of mind. He "let the cat out" and told them in confidence of his clandestine involvement within the "Irish Organisation". They could not believe they ears. They had thought they would initiate him to Breton nationalism but here was a man of action telling them the real fight, not an academic one.

Arvor started asking questions about Breton Renaissance. How did they see their goals? What had they done so far? What was the structure? What kind of struggle were they contemplating? He soon discovered Breton nationalism was an idyllic concept. They were men of passion, but they were navigating in the dark. Unlike the Scots and the Irish who had experienced violent oppression from the English Crown time and time again, the Bretons had not endured violent persecutions from the

French state since 1800, end of the Chouan war. The government in Paris had not forgotten the rebellion in support of the royalty and the province was always lagging behind in obtaining financial help. The region was backward compared with the rest of France; Brittany was kept as an underdeveloped entity. Arvor had his doubts. *Did he want to get embroiled in a nascent fight for independence? Furthermore, did they really want to be independent?*

Arvor was in his early forties, and although still young, he thought retiring in Brittany would not be too hard to contemplate. *Then what to do?* He was not going to be inactive, therefore getting involved in the Breton movement could be intellectually challenging. He vowed to immerse himself in the history and economy of the ex-independent Duchy.

Arvor went back to Brehat and decided to move out so he would not be so visible. The Lannion region, mainly Perros-Guirec would be his base for the near future. He stayed in a hotel on the main beach. He wanted to buy a house, but he needed funds to purchase it; indeed, he had to find a way to get money available without awakening unwanted notice about his real identity. He took a trip to Lausanne and saw the Swiss banker who administrated his finances there. They decided to create a Swiss based company to send the funds to France; the money from Arvor's account was transferred to the newly created company. Any sizable purchase was completed in the name of the Swiss firm, Arvor, under an assumed name, posed as the agent of the company. Three months later, a little manor was bought, it had a commanding view on the east bay looking over L'Anse de Perros, with Trelevern in the distance. He also had an excellent view of the north east towards Isle Tome.

Arvor thought intensely on the task of making Brittany a viable autonomy. He spent hours in quiet reflection. *Was it to be a clean break, or recognition by France granting some phony independence? Was the local population even willing or ready to assume such ideology? If the undertaking were to proceed, would it resemble a crusade? Would it emphasise the fact Brittany was an ancient society that had survived until the Twentieth Century, and show to the rest of the world* their *ancient customs could not be ignored? Had the Bretons the will to keep them alive? Was an armed force to be used, probably not? The time of the Chouannerie was over. Peaceful protest and economic paralysis could be an avenue, but was the population ready for financial hardship? Maybe not. Who should he trust... the clergy, some academics? Socialists and Communists were not into regionalism, they were internationalists. The right, or extreme right would be more receptive, but the danger was sinking in the burgeoning of fascism of Italy and Germany. Was a stealth presence with slogans written on buildings everywhere during the night, give the impression a secret army was rising?*

All his questions had partial answers. He also considered getting in touch with the cultural, nationalistic fringe. The people promoting the revival of the old language, traditions, and art were generally full of Breton pride and could even lean toward separatism. Arvor 's ideas cogitated in his head.

Resting on a settee in his living room, Arvor dozed off. The notion of an independent Brittany had filled his brain; he fell into a deep sleep. He dreamt about the old kingdom before it became a Duchy. He rode in silver armour upon a white horse. His hair was longer, and he held a white with black cross standard in his right hand. Village followed village, and every locality was full of people in peasant dress, either bowing to him or cheering and waving farming implements in the air. The overall feeling was one of joy... joy motivated by freedom. The scenes went on and on, they all had a rural background of small communities, local church and adjacent cemetery. The dream was somewhat repetitive. Arvor awoke puzzled and disorientated. He stood and stretched. His throat was dry, so he went to the kitchen and drunk from the tap with his cupped hands.

Chapter Thirty

However discreet Arvor tried to be with the meetings he had with Breton nationalists and people favourable for independence, he was not able to prevent his presence and activities from becoming conspicuous to the French local police, who in turn notified the regional authorities, and sooner or later it ended up with the French Secret Service. The initial tip-off was probably from some of the people he had met.

When news reached the headquarters of the secret service, they informed MI5 a British subject was meddling with a crowd favouring the breakup of Brittany from France. If a foreigner was involving himself in a movement seeking to do away with the central government of France, that said individual might have a past showing specialism in such activities. French ego was wounded—a foreigner involved in inciting secession was unbearable. Obviously, Arvor was not aware of any concern.

Once the respective agencies contacted each other, they had to decide upon the appropriate surveillance and apprehension procedure. Either the French would kidnap Arvor and deliver him to the British, or the Brits would act undercover while the French kept a blind eye. It was agreed the French would abduct Arvor, put him in a French Navy vessel and rendezvous with a Royal Navy boat offshore from Perros-Guirec in international waters. A surveillance was initiated and from it, the opportune moment to apprehend Arvor was when undertaking his morning constitutional for his paper and coffee at the café near the church.

Arvor was vigilant and knew there was a possibility of the British catching up with him. Anytime he heard English spoken, he put up his guard. He carried a *Beretta* handgun most of the time.

The road where Arvor lived was tranquil, any car crawling along would put him on alert. The abductors chose to use a van with a side sliding door camouflaged as a local delivery van so as not to alarm their prey in any way.

The day chosen for the kidnap was a Saturday. It was raining, the sky was dark-grey. Following his regular routine, Arvor was walking nonchalantly on the left side of the street, which was deserted as usual at that time of day. Suddenly, he heard a scratching of tyres, and saw a delivery van moving towards him. His deep-rooted reflexes came back to him in an instant, and they told him danger was coming towards him at high speed. He had expected such a moment for a while; it would be coming from the Brits or the American-Irish predictable retaliation. He reached for his Beretta and simultaneously removed the safety catch. From the sliding side door of the vehicle, now ten metres away and still moving, two men, with their faces covered, jumped out and rushed towards him, one of them held a white cloth in his hand. Arvor did not hesitate and shot the empty-handed man; the bullet reached him in the forehead. A second bullet entered the other man's head, and he fell backward. The van driver stepped on the accelerator, and before Arvor could avoid it, he was knocked down on the pavement. The driver stopped, leapt out of the vehicle and pumped three shells into Arvor's skull. Three bodies now lay momentarily in the street. The driver loaded them in the van. The confrontation had lasted less than a minute.

The van was driven to the local gendarmerie in Lannion, as previously planned. The driver explained the fiasco, and phone calls were made to the Paris headquarters of the French secret service. The van, and its cargo of dead bodies, arrived in Paris under escort. Arvor was identified correctly and then driven to a local morgue, duly kept under guard.

The British authorities were notified of the outcome of the deadly shootout in Brittany. They sniggered that the French could not do anything right. The corpse of the Celtic revolutionary was to be transferred to England and buried in an unmarked grave in a north London cemetery. As he no longer had family or assets in Britain, they suspected his possessions were hidden outside of the United Kingdom, but there was no lead. Former workers on Arvor's estates in Scotland did not produce much information.

However, in researching bank records in Scotland and England, agents managed to trace the Norwegian *chargé d'affaires*, but he would not cooperate, and there was nothing they could do. Once the Norwegian was alerted, he was uncertain how to proceed and what he should do with all the assets in Switzerland and Sweden. He knew Arvor's ideas and motivations, but he was at a loss as to whom to contact. He chose to wait and be the stealth keeper of the wealth left behind by the Celtic warrior.

With the removal of Arvor, the thin bloodline of that Celtic dynasty came to a tragic end. Having shaped the history of several corners of Europe, for more than two thousand years, there were no close relations or friends to appreciate the sadness of the event. There were, without doubt, some blood relatives in the village of Plumelec, (Treveleg in earlier times). Arvor's distant ancestors had married some of the residents; they were unaware of their being the last connection to Ervar.

Chapter Thirty-One

In the 1930's, France was still licking its wounds from the Great War. There was a realisation from nationalists, as well as the ordinary Breton, that being French came at a high price. The number of Breton men killed in the First World War was much higher than any other province in terms of percentages. Women had always indirectly micro-managed Brittany with the help of the clergy. There was also a sense it was the last region to benefit from the centralised help from Paris. The immigration took Bretons to Paris, Le Havre. Nantes was the only prosperous and dynamic town while Brest and Lorient provided harbours for the Navy.

Nationalism and concepts of separation started to show themselves more considerably. The people promoting the visions were an odd amalgam of royalists, heirs of the Chouannerie, and linguists in the protection of the Breton language and culture. Unfortunately, their model loosely followed the fascist movements in Europe and it caused grave concerns from moderates and the establishment.

Historically, the centralised government in Paris, if not an enemy, did nothing in the interests of Brittany. The *left* was influential in France, but not interested in listening to any regionalist argument. The *Parti Nationaliste* Breton and the *Breiz Atao* (Brittany Forever) were definitely going right and even extreme right. There was an element of racial exclusivity; they compared the Breton culture, history, character and origins, as different, if not purer than the rest of France. It did not have to be, but out of desperation, frustration, and impatience, a slippery slope was taking form. Unfortunately, the model attracted petty criminals and misfits. Compared with the independent movement of Ireland, this was rougher, neither intellectually mature nor cultured. The theorists at the top were on another level from the rank and files.

Plumelec was trilingual—Breton, French, and Gallo were all spoken. The idea of independence had not taken root. Peasant life was arduous and left little time for anything other than agricultural-working and survival. They knew they were Bretons but without any patriotic aspiration. The losses of their sons during the Great War made them think they were dependent on Paris, and France. They were subordinates, it was a burden, but they had no idea how to unload it. The frustration of some made them head towards an authoritarian path. The thought of radically forcing destiny took place; it required an active minority to show the way to the masses, using some demagogic slogans. These mistaken idealists thought the goals justified the means. In Brittany, the nationalist movement was not even a minority—the leaders were intellectuals, academics, and a few clergymen, none close to the reality of the life of an ordinary Breton. The population was simply trying to survive the aftermath of the Great War.

The "*debacle*" of June 1940 brought the Germans to Brittany. The harbours such as Brest, Lorient, and St Nazaire were real gems for the invaders, it gave them choice spots on the Atlantic Ocean and the Channel. Their submarines, especially, used the Breton facilities to their advantage.

The Bretons who abhorred invasion used many fishing boats to go to England where they were interned for a while until it was established they were not spies. At the opposite end of the spectrum, some nationalists fell for the promises of the Germans who were selling them a bill of goods by promoting independence inside the Reich. Those who joined set back any idea of autonomy for decades to come because autonomy meant collaboration. Some Bretons, under the label of being pro-independence, joined the SS. Some went to Russia, but many were used by the Gestapo to ferret out their compatriots in the Resistance.

The Vichy government, in a crippling act, decided to cut Nantes and the Loire delta from Brittany—a strange surgical action which remains unhealed today. Nantes and the rest of Brittany are still lobbying for the reattachment of the ancient capital of the Duchy to the rest of the province. So far, the pernicious act of Petain has not been rectified.

The coastal towns and the coastline in general, were of vital importance to the Germans, their navy could make a lot of trouble for the allies from Lorient, Brest and St Nazaire. Airports were also used to survey the English Channel and the Atlantic. The local Resistance recognised the significant source of intelligence they could transmit to the British. The latter also realised the potential; they established their own network filled with Breton resistants', even De Gaulle had no say in that set-up.

The 6th June 1944, and the massive Normandy landing gave considerable hope to occupied France. For the Allies, the liberation of Brittany was essential. The German naval power was concentrated there and a menace to all the Atlantic shipping routes. The German fighting was ferocious, it delayed the push toward the west by a month. The collaborators saw "the writing on the wall" and started heading east in the narrowing corridor for an escape towards Germany. For some, it was the pretext to go all out on acts of atrocities towards their compatriots. By that stage, the Allies were parachuting Free French commandos to help the local Resistance which was taking heart as the end of the dark days was in sight. However, some of the most intense fights took place during this time, and for many, it was the most bloodied part of the war.

Chapter Thirty-Two

In July of 1944, in the bar near the church of the village of Plumelec, it was time for the end of the working day aperitif. Some of the regulars—farm labourers, mechanics, local government blue collar and white collars employees—were either sitting at tables or the bar counter. There were no more than a dozen men sipping glasses of rough red wine. One or two were drinking Dubonnet, a strong quinine beverage with a very bitter taste. The chatter was about the ferocious fighting going on in the St Marcel area, north of Plumelec, where the Resistance and the Free French commando paratroopers had given a bloody battle to the Wehrmacht.

Everyone in the establishment was, as far as one could tell, not a member of the Resistance or a collaborator. Any clandestine activity one might have was kept secret; loose talk could kill. War and occupation by a foreign-armed force made people distrust one another. Denunciations to the occupiers were everyday occurrences.

One of the customers mentioned he might have seen some paratroopers near the hamlet of Cadoudal (native place of the Chouan leader) south west of Plumelec, and they were moving south towards a small agglomeration of farms on top of a wooded hill named Kerihuel.

Nobody will ever know who transmitted the conversation to the Breton SS and the Wehrmacht in Vannes. The grim reality was such that a full squad of Breton fascists in civilian clothes and a battalion of German soldiers were going door to door at about four o'clock in the morning. They forced the owner of the bar to open up and interrogated him for the name of the person who had mentioned seeing paratrooper activity. The bar proprietor said he could not remember, and they took him away.

Another group of the Breton fascists went to Cadoudal and made every household stand outside, including women and children. They lined up twelve men and threatened to shoot them all if they were refused to cooperate. Some did not know; some knew where they had heard or seen the French Commandos, but they would not say as they would be seen as informers for the rest of their lives. They knew deep in their hearts the end was near and they would soon be rid of those bastards.

Suddenly, three of the fascists started shooting and killed ten men. In the chaos of the bloodbath, two of the victims managed to run, jump over hedges then disappear in the fields. One of them ran towards Kerihuel, about two kilometres away, uphill. When he got there, he woke up everybody asking how he could get in touch with the commandos. He told them about the massacre at Cadoudal. The inhabitants had seen the commando camp three hundred metres west of the hamlet. There were also some scattered commandoes in the vicinity. It took ten minutes to alert some of them and members of the Resistance; they organised themselves to make a stand. Just as they were ready, a column of Breton fascists entered the hamlet and was confronted by an intense fire of rifles, automatic weapons and grenades. The militiamen reposted violently.

A full regiment of German soldiers, having left St Jean Brevelay, heard the fighting in the distance and hurried from the north west towards Kerihuel.

The Resistants and the Free French commandos had to fight on two fronts, from the east with the Bretons SS with whom fighting had begun, and very shortly from the north with the Wehrmacht. Within minutes, the German soldiers reached Kerihuel. The Germans set up a couple of heavy machine guns and started sweeping the edges, and hurling grenades. Heartened by the soldiers' arrival, the fascists broke cover and began to move forward; a few more of their men died.

The defenders had three dead. They were so overwhelmed in numbers, they did not know how long it would be before they were all killed. They were waiting for reinforcement from other Resistants disseminated in the countryside, but nothing was coming. Desperation was settling in—someone stood up and raised a white handkerchief. He likely presumed if he surrendered, it was only a small number of days before the allies reached the region. The move of their comrade shocked those still fighting. As the white flag bearer continued advancing towards the Germans, he was mauled down, riddled with bullets.

The inevitable happened, and the defenders came out with their hands high in a gesture of cease-fire demand. They wondered why nobody had come to their support. There were ten of them, two of whom were wounded and could not stand up. The Breton fascists asked the Germans to let them deal with the Resistants, pointing out they were better equipped to get information. The Germans acquiesced and left to deal with other pockets of insurgents. The Breton SS shot the wounded straight away, raising protests from the guerrillas. The able-bodied were lined up against one of the walls of the farm's building. The head of the group started to shoot at random with an automatic weapon, others joined in. All the victims suffered a cruel and undignified death. The murderers then left in the opposite direction from the Germans. They never thought for a moment their acts were atrocious and cowardly.

Of the presumed dead, one gentleman miraculously escaped the vile execution by bullet. Gabriel Le Breton, from Felgué, a hamlet of Plumelec, was a distant descendant of the long line of Celts who had left central Europe several millennia ago. He could not comprehend why he had been spared or by whom.

Gabriel Le Breton never married nor had any children, however, the blood of the ancient ancestors, though diluted, was within him and his siblings, Le Bretons of Plumelec.

Epilogue

The saga of the clan has spanned many centuries; many different Celtic tribes took different paths from western Europe to the four corners of the world.

The tribe within these pages never forgot, through many generations, where it came from and had no doubt as to its future path.

The bloodline took the following path—Bohemia, France, southern and western England, Wales, north western England, Brittany, England, Scotland, Ireland, America, and Brittany. Celtic ethnicity is the core which threads all these lands together. After all those centuries, cultures and behaviours, hold substantial similarities.

For nearly three thousand years of the Celtic migratory spread, their will to pass on their forefathers' knowledge has not waned.

Modern nations and governments have failed to constrain the Celtic spirit. Should the story of the Celtic people be considered relevant? Yes indeed. Their contribution to western European civilisation is colossal.

Theirs is a history of survival kept alive by ancestral endeavour and belief.

Fact or legend, it matters not; in Celtic, the two can mean the same.

Gwad Karentez in Breton:

"For the love of our blood heredity."

The Bloodline never perished and hopefully never will.

Too many have given their lives for the survival of the culture and civilisation.

About the Author

Yves Kerdal has his roots in the Morbihan region of Brittany and as far as he knows, his family have been there for at least a thousand years.

Yves was educated through the French public education system. He went to England where he achieved a BSc in Geology from Southampton University then worked as an exploration geologist for a large mining company in northern Canada, He then spent a year in Oxford and worked on a Master Diploma thesis. Circumstances of life made him become a proprietary trader in London and New York. His love of wide and wild spaces had him emigrate to Wyoming where he became an hotelier.

Yves' scientific enquiring mind made him explore the real history of Brittany and it led to his research of the Western Celts whom he sees as a forgotten race in the mix of modern civilisation.

www.ingramcontent.com/pod-product-compliance
Lightning Source LLC
Chambersburg PA
CBHW020335180726

47991CB00020B/1699